BLESSED

Abundantly

BOOK TWO OF THE WEST HOPE TRILOGY

MARY JEAN BONAR

Other books by this author:

Overflowing with Hope, 2008, Tate Publishing Company
Look to the Hills, 2012, Book One of the West Hope Trilogy, WestHope Publishing

The basis for The West Hope Trilogy begins with a restructuring
of the novel Overflowing with Hope

Printed in the United States of America.

ISBN: 978-1-7347977-2-5 (paperback)
ISBN: 978-1-7347977-3-2 (eBook)

WestHope Publishing, LLC
WELLSBURG, WV

"I will bless them and the places surrounding my hill.
I will send down showers in season;
There will be showers of blessing.
The trees of the field will yield their fruit and
The ground will yield its crops;
The people will be secure in their land.
They will know that I am the LORD."
Ezekiel 35:26-27a NIV

Contents

Acknowledgement

I give praise to my Father in Heaven for preparing me to write this Trilogy, and for strongly nudging me into doing so. All of life is a preparation for something. One should always be open to receive the message of what that "something" is. I strongly believe in the fact that each of us is here for a purpose in God's Kingdom. Christ left this world in our hands to follow His lead to continue the work here. I do my best with prayer and meditation to discover what I should do each day to fulfill the reason for my life here on this earth. I thank the Lord for life itself and for bringing about my love of music and writing which I believe are the tools I have been given to use in His Kingdom.

I thank my husband, Jim, for standing by, helping in every way, and tolerating my busyness apart from him. My living children, Carol, Russ, and Marianne have been very supportive and oft times participants in my efforts, and I love them and sometimes even appreciate their constructive criticisms. My grandchildren Lauren, Aaron, Kassidy, Wendy, Michael, Christopher, and Jonathan awaken my senses and help me to see a world that is often very different from the one I've always known, but quite interesting and energizing as well. We also have additions of sons and daughters in law who add bright perspectives to our fundamental thinking. Our youngest family members of the fourth generation bring much joy and add to the overall mix of our family life; for even youngsters offer precious things to consider, such as spontaneous giggles and splashing in water puddles. My appreciation is extended to each of these beloved ones for strengthening my desire to continue to be a worthy member of our wonderful family.

I wish again today that I could thank my parents, my grandparents, and my daughter, Diane for their love and for helping to shape my life, but that will have to wait until we meet again in heaven. To all of my aunts, uncles, and cousins; my friends over the years who have helped me along the way, and to members of my church family who really are true brothers and sisters, I thank God for each and every one of you.

To my readers: *"Look to the Hills"* had a significantly beautiful scene as the cover of that book. Thanks to our friends, Elaine and Dick Patton for keeping their farmland so perfectly beautiful and for giving me permission to photograph the pasture and the rising hills as the cover. The road we drive many times a week looks just like the picture of this book. We see the clouds forming as so very beautiful, don't we? The farmers are abundantly blessed that they got that hay in before the next rain. I hope you, the reader, will like *this* book, *Blessed Abundantly*. Some writings that I especially enjoy are within. Thanks for your loving support always.

Coming to America

Who was more excited? Claire was coming from France into Pittsburgh today. Karen and Meghan Lang had Claire's picture with them so that they could identify her. Spotting her, however, would not be a problem. They had her image imprinted on their hearts and minds. They noticed that there were many others waiting for a student as well. They tried to relax by entering into conversation with others in the waiting room of the airport.

Their mother, Kathy, watched the girls as the door opened for the arrival of those coming to America. There were at least sixty young French students coming down the passageway.

"There she is!" Karen exclaimed. And sure enough, it was Claire. She was beautiful, as they knew she would be. Her dark hair was longer now, extending down her back, almost to her waist. Fashionably dressed, she wore a blue pleated skirt that rested above her knees with leggings the color of persimmon and carried a large shoulder bag. Karen and Meghan were jumping up and down, calling her name. She heard them and looked their way. She smiled, waved, and indicated that she had to stay with her group for the time being. They acknowledged that they understood, and Claire moved along with the students to where Deborah was standing.

Deborah, Kathy's sister, was the one who would be welcoming Claire and all the students to America. She had been participating in the arrangements for exchange students for a few years, and as a high school French teacher, she was especially valuable in the role. She was the student's first impression, and her family was proud of her and the warm words of welcome she extended to the group.

Deborah called attention to the guidelines for the visit and emphasized the importance of speaking English as much as possible. After all, their parents were expecting them to learn from the culture here, and they had all studied English for six years or more. This was to be part of their educational process.

"But above all," Deborah said, "enjoy your new families and have fun! I'm going to call each one of you forward to be introduced to your new family." She proceeded to announce the name of the individual who stepped forward as his or her host family came to greet them. It was a joy to behold, especially for the families. The students seemed to be a little shy and reserved. Claire was certainly lovingly received and warmly welcomed, and when she realized that Deborah was a part of her new family, she managed a little smile as her nervousness eased a little.

I hope this is going to be a good experience, she thought. *These people seem to be very nice.* Although she continued to be apprehensive, she managed to appear pleased to be there.

She was at least relieved that her host family and the others in the airport did not emerge as rude and totally unsophisticated as she expected. On the streets of France, when there were American tourists, most could easily be detected by their brashness and sloppy attire and seemed to be more concerned with pushing their way along and being dressed for *la bataille.* The French would speak about them and say, "Look out, the Americans are here."

Her instructor in France had told the students who were to be traveling to America this year that not all Americans were the same as those they were used to seeing. Nevertheless, she and the others were skeptical.

Claire had also been somewhat afraid to be in America. The television and the newspapers had been presenting turmoil in America, and she was certain that she would encounter racial violence in the cities and elsewhere. The instructor had done his best to dilute that concept and reduce their fears; however, that form of information was measured out daily, and it was difficult for the students to not be afraid and guarded.

They had talked among themselves about how to come to grips with challenging situations that they would likely encounter in America. Claire personally had difficulty understanding why her parents would send her to a country where, possibly, another revolution could take place. She would not question her parents. Consequently, they had no idea that she was anything but excited with the opportunity to see America.

She looked around the airport, expecting to see the military everywhere with large weaponry in hand. She saw only a few security guards, making their way through the crowds without force. She knew they were carefully checking everyone, but they were not heavily armed, nor was their presence threatening to anyone . . . at least not at the moment.

I wish I hadn't come, she thought. *In a few minutes, all of my friends will be gone from me, and I will be alone with the American family. How can we possibly have anything in common? These trips are supposed to give us some understanding of people from other countries. Why couldn't I have gone to Holland, Ireland, or Italy? I didn't want to come here!*

This family told me they live in a log home. I've seen pictures of those cabins. We'll all be crowded up into a small space and have no privacy at all. My family is well established in the aristocracy. This family should see where I live!

She was polite and agreeable with her host family—these commoners—and would continue to be so, no matter what she actually thought of them. Her parents would expect no less of her.

ϓϓϓ

When the family drove up to the house, Claire was completely bewildered. It did not look like Abraham Lincoln's log cabin. She could never have imagined a house made entirely of logs to be so large.

Prince bounded to the car to meet them, and Claire was very happy that there was a dog in the family. There were several dogs on her family's estate, and she loved each one of them. Prince was likeable in every way, and they became friends immediately. A dog can warm a room or a heart when nothing else can.

They went inside. The house was warm and inviting and surprisingly efficient with running water, bedrooms . . . luxurious in a strange sort of way. The family welcomed her into their home and walked her through the main part of the house.

As she climbed the stairway to the loft, it seemed she was in a fantasy. No house she had ever been in before had a loft. She likened it to the balcony in a theater; however, this "balcony" had rooms.

Meghan was excited to let her know that she was giving Claire her room for her visit. "It's very peaceful up here and cozy, and the bathroom is right here beside it. Come on, I'll show you where Karen and I will be sleeping."

Claire followed the girls as they introduced her to her surroundings. Later in the day, when Greg came home from work, all three girls rushed down from the loft to see him.

"Daddy, this is our new friend, Claire."

Claire looked up at the six-foot, three-inch man with a very broad smile and warm nature. She extended her hand to him, and he welcomed her to their home. He said he would be preparing dinner in a short while, which did not seem unusual at all to Claire.

The meal prepared by *le père* was delicious, and she ate more than she intended. It was casually served at the kitchen table, which she thought rather crude. The kitchen was for dining only by the hired help in her home. Obviously, there were no hired help here.

Each person cleared her portion of the table, and she insisted that she would do the same. She had been instructed to follow whatever was the common practice in her host home, and so she would. *This is only for one month. I can do it,* she thought.

No one could have predicted how much she would love Prince, but then everyone loves Prince. He decided to adopt Claire immediately. He curled up at her feet at dinnertime and followed her upstairs at bedtime. Kathy called him to come back downstairs, but Claire asked if he could please remain with her.

"Of course, Claire, if you don't mind having Prince with you, that will be fine," Kathy said, thinking that perhaps Prince gave Claire some comfort in her strange environment.

Claire was very appreciative of having Prince with her. She sat on the edge of the bed and said, "*Allez,* Prince."

He understood her and came to her immediately. She began to speak to him in her native language, telling him how handsome he was and that they should become very good friends.

Prince looked at her and understood every word. He was a remarkable dog!

It gave Claire comfort to speak in French, and Prince enjoyed it as well. She told him about her home and her dogs there and how beautiful her country was. He wanted to know more, but she became very sleepy.

"*Bonne nuit*," she said as Prince curled up on the floor beside her. She closed her eyes and was soundly asleep in minutes.

ᕍᕍᕍ

The next morning was one of the most beautiful days ever—a perfect day to explore the fields and outer areas of the house. Claire and the girls relaxed a bit with one another and began giggling and talking excessively throughout the day.

Karen and Claire were almost the same age. They discussed their schools, studies, and activities. It was amazing that they both seemed to have the same opinions about much of what they were learning. Karen was impressed that Claire was required to learn many languages, especially English.

"In America, we can select a foreign language and usually study that one for two or three years. I have chosen French but would be embarrassed to speak your language with you. I have only had one year so far. You speak English very well," Karen said.

"Thank you very much. I have studied this for six years."

Meghan returned to the house to give the older girls an opportunity to spend time discussing things of mutual interest. She really didn't want to do that, but her mother had given her "orders" before they went outside.

Karen asked her about her home life, and Claire, not revealing anything more than she had to, touched on the fact that she was an only child and lived in the country. She did say that they usually vacationed every summer, and her parents would be arranging for her to visit other countries over the next two summers. It was a cultural experience for her to have a better understanding of the global scene.

Claire enjoyed the walk. It was very quiet. She wondered how far they were from other houses but did not ask. She would take her time and would learn from experiences instead of asking too many questions.

Janine and John walked over to the Langs later in the afternoon to meet Claire and would have dinner with the family. Prince met them and led them to the backyard where the family was setting up for an American tradition.

Karen introduced her lovely guest to her grandparents, and Claire extended her hand as pleasantries were exchanged.

What a lovely girl, thought Janine.

Janine, Karen, and Claire sat on a bench and talked awhile. Janine could sense that Claire was uneasy even though her English was impeccable.

She needs time, thought Janine. *Kathy's family is the best at making someone feel comfortable. It won't take long.*

Claire and Karen went to the house together to gather some items that Greg needed.

The two girls were talking away, and Janine sensed that they would shortly be best friends.

Soon Greg was grilling, Kathy and the girls were carrying food out to the picnic tables, and there was excitement in the air. Their special guest was about to experience her first American barbecue—a truly perfect idea.

Claire would write home about this dinner! Greg cooked up the best hamburgers and hot dogs anyone ever had. Claire thought the meal was delicious, including potato salad and baked beans, which she ate there for the first time in her life. They finished the meal with good old American apple pie and ice cream. Everyone thought the food was delicious, and it was fun and a bit of an icebreaker for Claire.

How pleasant to be sitting out in the yard to eat, Claire thought. *I'm going to request that we try eating out in one of the gardens at home some time—or at least on the veranda.*

It was an ideal evening for the picnic from any viewpoint. The weather had remained picture-perfect throughout the day, birds were chirping, flower gardens were in full bloom, and the yard was sheltered into complete privacy by trees and beautifully appointed bushes.

The tables were covered with red-and-white-checkered tablecloths, and they ate from Styrofoam plates. She tried to spell "Styrofoam" in her letter to her mother but didn't think she did so correctly.

She took picture after picture of the family, the table, of Greg and his grill, and the surroundings. By the time evening came and they all went indoors, everyone seemed to be more relaxed with one another. Claire discovered that she was smiling without straining to do so.

When she and Prince went up to bed, she had a fine conversation with him. He agreed that they had a rather nice day today.

As she continued to speak French, she told him that Karen was a very bright girl, which was not news to him. He always did think so.

Prince put his head on her lap and comforted her as she confided to him that she missed her mother.

She was thankful for Prince and found that she wanted to warm up to the family as well. As they were both preparing to go to sleep, she vowed to Prince that she would do her best to accept her fate here and work harder at having appreciation for the family that had welcomed her so sincerely. He accepted that and went straight to sleep.

She finished her letter to her mother and drifted off to sleep as her lips bent into a soft smile.

2

A Woodland Experience

It was a beautiful morning as John appeared out of the woods from behind their home. His steps were swift and nimble, and as he approached the back of the house, he called Janine.

"Honey, you have to come to the woods with me. I have found lilies in bloom all along the little creek there. Come and see!"

"John, I'm afraid of the woods," she called from the upper deck.

"You don't have to be afraid. There's nothing there to hurt you, and it's cool and beautiful under the shelter of the large tree branches. Come on . . . I'll be right beside you. I want you to see the lilies."

Fear gripped Janine as she instantly recalled being lost in the woods as a child. She had been with a Girl Scout troop and innocently wandered from the others. When she suddenly realized that she was alone, the wooded area seemed to press upon her. The trees were overpowering and she didn't know where she was. It was only moments before she was found, but those few frightening moments have prevented her from ever entering into the suffocating captivity of any wooded area.

"John, I don't think I can do it."

"Please, honey, come and try. If you become too frightened, we won't go forward."

Janine wanted to go and decided that maybe she could. She put on an old pair of shoes and joined up with him in the backyard.

The closer she got to the mass of trees, the more nervous she became. John took her hand and kept assuring her she would be fine. She felt like a little child and truly ridiculous as she tried to remain calm and trust in John to lead her through. Everything closed in. There was nothing but trees and undergrowth.

John was compassionately understanding and helpful, and she continued to lean upon him for courage. A deer bounded up suddenly, and both the animal and the humans were startled. Janine gripped John tightly at the unexpected interruption yet appreciated the beauty and gracefulness of this creature in its natural habitat. She drew in a deeper breath, pleasurably inhaling a new fragrance of nature's ever-changing subsistence.

Janine was thinking, *This is a completely contradictory environment for me—frightening yet fascinating. I can do this for John as long as I have him with me.*

When they moved on down to the creek, the trees opened up to the light, and Janine was much happier and more relaxed. John still held her hand and took them along the creek bank a few yards . . . and there they were—hundreds of gorgeous auburn-to-orange lilies.

"What do you think?" John asked.

"I can't believe it . . . John, they are beautiful. No wonder you wanted to bring me here. Let's go over and smell them."

It was a little muddy underfoot, but they were careful. They found themselves surrounded by the flowers and bees and butterflies, giving them a feeling of God's intended Paradise. The creek water was lightly playing a melody over the rocks, and the buzzing of the bees and the chirping of the birds were in perfect harmony.

Janine had a lump in her throat as she looked at John and said, "Thank you, John. If you hadn't insisted, I would have missed this beautiful moment."

He hugged her and said, "It would never have meant the same to me without being able to share it with you."

They stood there for quite some time without speaking, enjoying the peaceful setting. John asked Janine if she would like for him to dig up some of the flowers and replant them in their yard.

"That would be wonderful, John. Why don't we have the girls come along to see the flowers with us, and they can help you dig and carry?"

"Good idea, but do you think it would be all right now that Claire is there?"

"I think so. I'll call Kathy and ask her."

When they got back into the house, Janine called Kathy, and she thought it would be a good experience for all three girls.

She arranged for them to come over in their scruffy clothes the next day and enter into an adventure with the grandparents.

ฯฯฯ

The girls skipped along together as they came to Grandma's house, looking every bit the part of diggers and gatherers. Claire was wearing a pair of Meghan's old sport shoes and some clothes that Janine recognized as Karen's.

"Good morning," said Janine as she and John stood in the doorway.

"*Bonjour, Grand-mère. Bonjour, Grand-père*," the three responded in unison.

"Are you ready to go exploring?" John asked.

"*Oui.*"

"Come inside while I gather up some gloves for us and *Grand-père* gets his tools from the garage."

While their shoes were not yet muddy, the girls showed Claire around the house. They met the grandparents in the yard, and off they went to explore the woods. None of the three actually had been in these woods before, so it was a new experience for all of them. They were discussing the wilderness and what they might encounter as they walked over the terrain.

John had been the leader of the way, and Karen took the responsibility of keeping Grandma on her feet. Not a single one of them had any idea that Janine feared being there. Arriving at the creek, they wanted to immediately go wading, and John and Janine saw no reason why they shouldn't. The girls left their shoes on so they wouldn't cut themselves on the rocks or anything else that might be hidden in the moving waters. They marched along, laughing and carrying on for a while. The time eventually came to begin the project.

They found it harder to walk now with wet shoes, but they didn't care one bit.

Someone decided to count the flowers. After counting to ninety, they decided there were at least two hundred, and they didn't need to count anymore! John began to dig, and he instructed the girls to place them carefully onto the papers he had brought along. Carrying the small packages through the foliage was tedious work with weighted-down wet shoes, but no one complained. It had been a great experience for everyone. Janine was very pleased that she had been able to participate in the joyous adventure. Perhaps she will someday overcome this lifelong fear of hers.

John offered to give the girls a lift home, and they were grateful because of the struggle to walk in the shoes.

Plodding to the house, they were talking excitedly about the fun they had with the grandparents. Kathy was eager to hear all about it. She waved to her father as the girls removed their shoes. They had to go around to the back of the house and hose off all the mud before Kathy would permit them to enter. They certainly understood.

At bedtime, Prince was eager to hear all about how Claire could have been so muddy. She told him that she had a very interesting day surrounded by flowers. Her words about the girls were affectionate, and Prince responded lovingly. She laughed when she described that it was actually fun walking in squishy, muddy shoes. Prince wagged his tail as though he wished he could have been there with them.

Perhaps it was a good match for her to be in this place. She would definitely learn about everyday life from a completely new aspect, and that was indeed what she was sent to do.

Her resignation pleased Prince, and he stretched out on the floor as she bid him "*bonne nuit.*"

3

O, Say Can You See?

The Fourth of July was a great day to appreciate the "good ol' USA." Claire sang "God Bless America," heard Lee Greenwood's "God Bless the USA," and stood for the "Star-Spangled Banner." Deborah and Bob joined the family and brought Claire a shirt in red, white, and blue with firecrackers exploding all over it. The evening of the fourth, when they were all on the banks of the Point in Pittsburgh, watching a spectacular presentation of fireworks over the three rivers, Claire unpredictably felt the thrill of being an American.

She had been positive that there would be demonstrations and unrest on the streets of Pittsburgh, although she did not mention it. The drive into Pittsburgh was beautiful and exciting. They had parked the car in a parking lot quite a distance from the celebrations, but walking gave them all an opportunity to see a lot more of the city.

Claire hid her nervousness as she peered from side to side and around corners, expecting something vile to happen. When she finally realized that all was well, she began to silently question all the reports she had heard about America. As they went through the day and night, her anxieties decreased, and she had a wonderful time. She would wear her new shirt with pride.

On the seventh, she met up with her fellow travelers who were aglow with happiness. They all shared their experiences with one another. Kathy and Greg noticed that Claire was talking excitedly with her French peers, and everyone in the large room seemed to be quite happy and energized at that point.

Soon the band was set up, and the members of it were young and loud—just what the French and American teens enjoyed. There was no holding back as dancing got underway and strobe lights flashed. Everyone danced around with whoever was at hand, and they interacted eagerly as though they had known one another forever. Kathy was convinced that music and rhythm was indeed a universal language.

The young people had a wonderful evening, and the parents were happy as well, even though the music was louder than they could enjoy. The family talked all the way back home, and the parents suggested that everyone rest up during the next day because they would be leaving for a trip the following morning.

They all fell into bed exhausted and did rest the next day, except to pack for their trip. The following morning, they were traveling the American highways. Claire tried not to miss a thing as she kept asking questions and looking out of the car windows.

First, they went to Washington, DC, for three days, on to Williamsburg, Virginia, and then two days at Bush Gardens!

The Langs realized that even though Washington, DC, was beautiful and magnificently designed, it could not be compared with Versailles and Paris. Claire disagreed. She was very impressed and thrilled to have been at the center of American laws and government. She had seen the images time and time again on television and would now be able to identify the buildings.

There were those who were demonstrating about something near the Washington Monument, but it was peaceful—unlike other demonstrations Claire had seen on television.

Looking at the Capitol Building, Claire thought about all the news reports she had seen in France and also on American television about the disgruntled arguments constantly occurring between US government officials. She felt that if they couldn't get along, how could they possibly manage the entire country? She hoped to discuss this with the Langs someday if she ever felt more at ease to do so.

She loved Williamsburg. She had seen nothing like it ever! And what girl in the whole world would not enjoy Bush Gardens? She rode the roller coasters and double loop over and over.

They were traveling on Bastille Day, and Claire told the family of the way they celebrated their French holiday, which she said is *Fête, de la Fèdèration*, to celebrate the French Revolution.

"Perhaps you could visit France to celebrate our holiday with my family. You could see the fireworks in Paris from the Eiffel Tower. Our fireworks are beautiful, but perhaps not so much so as were those in Pittsburgh," Claire said.

No one could say yes or no at that point. It was a generous invitation, and they would remember it.

They welcomed the peace and quiet that the house offered. Prince was glad to see them all and demonstrated his joy to every one of them, including Claire. She flopped down on the floor with him, and they tussled and rolled around together in pure delight.

Claire had a long talk with Prince that night.

"Prince, I have missed you," she spoke in her beautiful native tongue. "You are such a beautiful dog and a good friend." He wagged his tail in response.

"I came to this country with many misconceptions. Don't tell your family, but I thought they would never live up to standards high enough for me. What a prude I was!

"I was so wrong. They and most Americans I have met are kind, generous, and loving people. It is such a tragedy that the news reports twist things around so that those of us who are in other countries are becoming more and more distrusting of Americans. I am going to do everything I can to spread the word that your people—and dogs!—are perhaps the finest this world has to offer."

Prince thought *she* was one of the best. As she spoke, she kept looking at him and petting him. He would listen to her as long as she wanted to talk. Prince was her first real friend in America and had helped her through those early days. The bond was set. They would be friends for life.

When the time arrived to say good-bye to Prince, Claire actually cried. Prince consoled her once again. She held on to the hope that she would see him again someday.

The day for Claire's departure came much too soon for her and for everyone else. In the hearts of those who shared her time in America, she would always be a real part of their family, and hopefully, she would come back again.

Janine and John would not stay home this time but went to the airport with the family to say *au revoir*. It was touching and difficult for all the exchange students and their host families. Warm farewells could be heard throughout the airport as the families sent the students back to France.

Deborah had told Kathy's family that the main reason for the exchange was to promote peace among peoples of all nations. It was a great concept, and the program generally did accomplish its goal of doing just that. There wasn't a better way to understand others than to share quality time together. Claire had come to a good place to learn of the sincerity, generosity, and loving nature of the people of the United States. She would go home and spread the word, one by one.

The reserved manners of the families sensed when the students arrived had completely vanished. There were hugs, tears, and heartfelt wishes for another time to be together. The Langs were already planning for the days when Claire would return. They would definitely stay in touch and take advantage of any opportunity to be together in the future.

4

A Basket of Neighborliness

Janine answered the knock at the front door. There stood the most beautiful young man she had ever seen. "Tall, dark, and handsome" might appropriately describe him but would not do him justice. He had glisteningly curly, dark-brown hair, expressively warm brown eyes, and an irresistible smile that drew in two beautifully placed dimples.

"Hello!" she said.

"Hello! My name's Tony. Tony Detelle. Welcome to the neighborhood!" He extended his hand.

She clasped his hand. "How do you do, Tony? Thank you. I'm Mrs. Stephens."

"Mrs. Stephens, my grandparents have sent over some food for you. It's in the car. So are my grandparents. Would you like to meet them?"

"Yes. Yes, I would." She went over to a very nice automobile—maybe a Lincoln—maybe not. She didn't really know one car from another.

In the backseat was a woman and in the front passenger seat, apparently her husband. When Janine walked toward the car, "Grandfather" got out and opened the door for his wife. They looked very happy and approached her warmly.

"This is my grandfather, Mario Detelle . . . and this is my grandmother, Sophia Detelle . . . This is Mrs. Stephens." They shook hands—Grandfather first. He was not as tall as Tony and had balding rather gray hair. She was mesmerized by his eyes, which were exactly like Tony's—beautifully brown and still with the same youthful-looking spark.

Mr. Detelle was smiling warmly. He shook Janine's hand with his right hand and covered her hand over with the other. He was nodding and said, "Pleased to meet you."

"Thank you. It's very nice to meet you also."

She turned to Mrs. Detelle. *What an attractive woman!* Even though she was probably in her seventies, she was beautiful. Janine always thought Italians were the most beautiful people on earth . . . perhaps because her mother's mother was Italian.

"How do you do, Mrs. Detelle?"

"I'm-a no speak-a da English too much," she said.

"That's fine. Don't worry about that . . . Please . . . I'm so happy to meet you."

Janine turned to Tony. "Where do you live?"

"We live toward West Hope a little ways. It's the house up on the hill with the pillars at the foot of the drive."

Good grief! The BIG house! It is one of those modern homes with lots of rooms and outside lights, thought Janine.

"Well, won't you come in?"

"Na, na! We just want'a you to have somet'ing from us to say we hope you happy here."

"That is just so nice of you. But please come on inside."

They decided that would be all right and appropriate, so Tony gathered up a nice basket, and Janine led them in through the front door to the kitchen.

"Here, we'll put the basket on the island. I'll call my husband—John!"

"Yes?"

"Can you come up please? We have company!"

He was so surprised and came rushing up the stairs. She introduced the Detelles to him and asked them if they would sit down. She would fix some coffee.

That was satisfactory with everyone, and they had a very pleasant but short visit. It was absolutely delightful! What lovely people. So mannerly and polite, and they were genuine in their desire for the Stephenses to feel welcome in the community.

Their son, Anthony, owns the house and had his parents move in with them. When Mario and Sophia came to America, Mario went to work in the coal mines.

"Anthony—he no wanted to do work in the mines, so he learn how to make a good business. He say he work on top-a da ground. That's-a good," Mario said.

The Stephenses learned that Anthony and his wife, Geonna, have three children and Tony is the youngest.

Tony said he is in his final year in high school. John asked him if he knew their granddaughter, Karen Lang, who is a sophomore. Tony said he knew her but wasn't sure if they had met.

They all had coffee. Mrs. Detelle said, "You have a nice-a kitchen. Very good."

"Thank you. We're very happy with it." She was totally overwhelmed by this remarkable visit. How special of them to come by! No one had done that. *Does anyone really welcome anyone anymore?*

"I'll take the food from the basket, and you can take the basket back with you," she said.

Mrs. Detelle said, "No, no! That's-a fine. You keep-a da basket. It's-a for you."

They were leaving. "You come over to see us sometime," Mr. Detelle said. "We would like-a to have you come see us." Mr. Detelle had been out into the world and had done much better with his English. Mrs. Detelle had stayed in most of the time, speaking mostly Italian to her son and husband.

Tony opened the car doors for his grandparents. He had nice manners and treated them with the utmost respect. *This boy is being brought up well.* Janine and John were both sensitive to his treatment of his elders.

John said the car was a Lincoln. Anthony had certainly done well for himself. They wondered what he did for a living. Whatever it was, capitalism worked!

They stood in the driveway as the Detelles left, feeling uplifted by the unexpected visit. As they walked back to the kitchen, they could smell the Italian sauce permeating the air. They could hardly wait to open the basket! Mmm, mmm! It was baked rigatoni! And there was freshly baked bread, which was always the best part of any meal for Janine.

"Oh my gosh! This is fantastic. Let's eat!" Janine said.

ᖌᖌᖌ

Karen answered the telephone. "Hi, Karen. It's Grandma. I wanted to talk with you."

"Hi, Grandma. You wanted to talk with me?"

"Yes. I wanted to tell you that we had a visitor today. It was Tony Detelle. Do you know him?"

"Do I know him? My goodness, yes. He's the most popular boy in the whole school! What on earth was he doing at your house?"

"Well, he lives just down the road, you know."

"Of course, I know . . . In that great big beautiful house on the hill. Oh my gosh. I can't believe he came to your house. Was he selling something?"

"No. Actually, he brought us something. His grandmother made us some baked rigatoni and bread to welcome us to the neighborhood, and Tony and his grandparents came and brought that and visited a while."

"Wow! They didn't come here when *we* moved in. What did he say?"

"He said he knew you."

"He knows me? I don't believe it. How would he have any idea who I am? He is always with a bunch of friends, and everyone wishes *they* were his friend, I can tell you that. He's a fine student—probably valedictorian—and is the big-time basketball star. He'll most likely go on to play basketball for some well-known college."

"Hmmm. I don't know about all of that, but I was very impressed with his politeness and manners."

"Mom wants to talk with you."

"Okay, sweetie."

"Hi! What's up?"

"I was telling Karen that we had a real nice visit this afternoon from the Detelles, who brought us a basket of welcome-to-the-neighborhood food. It was Tony and his grandparents. Do you know the family?"

"Yes. Everybody knows them, Mother. They live in that big house down the road a ways. Mr. Detelle, Tony's father, owns a meat packing business."

"Well, I wondered . . . Are you going to church tomorrow?"

"Yes. I was going to call you and see if you want to go with me. It's really a small church, Mother. I don't know what you'll think of it, but the people are very nice."

"Yes, I'll go with you. John and I have decided not to drive to Center Church anymore, and the other churches between here and there are just not working out for us. I'm actually feeling kind of low about it all right now. Maybe being with you would help."

"Okay. I'd like to go a little early because I want to talk with the lay minister about the hymns he would like before church begins. I'll stop by for you at ten fifteen. Okay?"

"Okay. See you then."

Janine had been almost ill with sadness. Never had she felt such depression. Every time they entered a church, she had hoped that maybe there was something there for her to begin anew, but so far, she had obviously not found the right church.

$$\curlyvee \curlyvee \curlyvee$$

Kathy and the girls were there on time. John said he would most certainly go with her. He had decided to leave Center Church with Janine, therefore, had resigned the session. There had been too many questions but not enough answers. It would be better for both of them if they worked through all of this side-by-side.

The little church was actually within walking distance. She had walked past it several times. It must have been built a long time ago and had very little maintenance lately. The cemetery had some old tombstones, and at one time, this church was, in all probability, the only church anyone could get to by foot or carriage. She envisioned church suppers and lawn gatherings from days gone by. Now there were many churches, and people most likely preferred a denominational church anyway. She did too, but who knows?

It was the normal-looking, one-room church, needing paint. It had a steeple of sorts and six steps leading to the front door. Someone had hung a wreath on it. Maybe it was Kathy. She would do that.

They entered into a tiny, entryway and opened up the door to the sanctuary. There didn't seem to be anyone there, and there were about ten rows of pews divided by an aisle in the middle. Up front was a pulpit on an elevated floor and a piano to the left. Three chairs were on the pulpit platform.

The lay minister came right behind them and greeted Kathy and her family. Kathy introduced Mr. Dawson to Janine and John, and the girls indicated a pew where they might be sitting. They sat and picked up a hymnbook. It was not one she had ever used, which was hard to believe. She had quite a collection. Anyway, it appeared to be quite old and was probably donated by another church at some point in time.

Janine looked around. The windows were frosted, the floors were bare, and the boards on the walls were unpainted clapboards. Why was Kathy here? Did the Lord lead her here, or did she just figure, *Why not?* She had told Janine that they needed her at the piano, so perhaps she had decided it was something she could do.

A few other parishioners came in. They were so curious with the new people sitting there, that they couldn't contain themselves. They rushed right over to meet them. They were still jabbering when Kathy was playing the prelude. Janine wanted to shush them. She always did think that it was rude for people to be talking during the prelude. To her, it was the opening of the worship service and a time of preparation for the congregation, not a time to talk louder and louder. She tried to be polite, even though she was annoyed.

Of course, she didn't find the opportunity to prepare herself. The people didn't even want to stop talking when the preacher said "Good morning!"

Finally, they did settle down. She grabbed John's knee, and he knew she was not where she wanted to be. *Well, the Lord would have a message for them so they had just better listen,* he thought.

The opening hymn was "Shall We Gather at the River." Janine knew this one, but her congregation had never sung it. It was rather refreshing to her actually. She couldn't hear many others singing, except the lady behind her who sounded more like a foghorn than anything else. She apparently thought she was an alto but couldn't locate the part. She kept singing anyway.

The minister cleared his throat—*ahem*—and read John 14:15-20:

> If you love me, you will obey what I command.
> And I will ask the Father, and He will give you
> another Counselor to be with you forever—the
> Spirit of Truth.
> The world cannot accept Him, because it neither
> sees Him nor knows Him.
> But you know Him, for He lives with you and will
> be in you.
> I will not leave you as orphans; I will come to you.
> Before long, the world will not see me anymore,
> but you will see me.

Because I live, you also will live.

On that day you will realize that I am in my Father,

and you are in me,

And I am in you.

Janine wanted to shout "Amen!"

John wanted to too. *This is a message for us.*

The minister raised his eyes from the Bible and cleared his throat. "Now then, some of you might be feeling all alone today." *Ahem.* "Perhaps it is you." *Ahem.* "This scripture is very comforting, isn't it?" *Ahem.* "Love and obey. *Ahem.* "That's what Jesus Himself is saying." *Ahem.* "Love and obey." *Ahem.* "You know that old hymn?" *Ahem.* "Well—*ahem*—we're going to sing that one today, aren't we, Kathy?" *Ahem.*

"But before we do—*ahem*—we need to continue to see what will result—*ahem*—what will be the result of our loving—*ahem*—and our obedience."

The poor fellow clears his throat with every sentence. How sad. How distracting! What is he trying to talk about? I don't know. I have counted thirteen times of clearing so far—now fourteen, John was thinking.

Eighty-seven throat clearings later, they stood to sing, "Trust and Obey." It wasn't "love" and "obey" after all—it was "trust" and "obey." *Oh well. It's a good old hymn anyhow. I'll get more out of singing this than I could possibly have gotten out of that sermon. I feel really sorry for that fellow. He probably wants to be a minister, and there is no way he will ever be able to get the message across. Did he feel called by*

God to do this? Can we ever absolutely know when we have found the calling? Oh Lord, please help me to know. Please, Lord. Please! Janine prayed all through the first stanza. Kathy was looking at her, wondering why she wasn't singing.

She joined in finally, and even the lady behind didn't do too badly on this one. Mr. Dawson was waiting in the back to shake everyone's hand. He said he hoped they would all return next week. Janine didn't respond one way or the other, but she knew for sure she would not be coming back. She felt really bad about her attitude. It wasn't right. She should not be so picky. After all, Mr. Dawson was a good fellow and trying his best. *I can't help it . . . I can't help it!*

She was in tears in the car. John felt sorry for her and knew that she was struggling with herself. When Kathy got in, she immediately noticed that Janine was crying.

"Mother, are you all right?"

"Sweetheart, I love you so much. You are a much better person than I am. I think you are so wonderful to come to this church and offer your services when you have to listen to a sermon like that."

"Mother, I do not get much out of it, I'll tell you the truth. Actually, I think I've been too lazy to search out a church that would be better for me. I should, really. Those few people there need to face up to closing the doors. They are just hanging on, and I'm helping them do it. I really do believe that it's coming very soon. If I didn't go there, they probably would finally resolve this. I guess it's something I need to pray about, instead of doing what's easy for me.

"Please don't think I'm some kind of saint. I sure am not. I wish I were, but my *raison d'être* is not in response to the Lord's calling or even His suggestion."

"Well, you are a wonderful person for sure. I'm sorry, sweetheart. I won't be going back next week."

"Mother, I understand. I do . . . I probably won't be going there much longer anyway."

5

A to Z

Francine and Lawrence were back from their wonderful vacation. Francine was back at the organ each Sunday and was really happy to be there after her extended and lighthearted break. She and Lawrence were still hoping to return to Florida by early November at the latest but would be patient in the findings.

"It's nice to have Francine and the choir back. The young man did a fine job with the hymns, but the worship service seemed to struggle along," said Iola.

"Well, summer's almost over. Are you going to get away, Iola?"

"I won't have the time, Harriet. Having this bunion removed is going to be my main concern."

"I hope you have a really good doctor. You're going to have to have some help after the operation. They say it takes about six weeks to actually get back on your feet."

"I know. That's why I've been putting it off so long, but it's come to the place now that I can't get around in decent shoes. I think I'll just go to the Continuous Care Center following the surgery and stay there until all is well again. Rachael is there also. So I might be able to be with her at times."

They had discussed Rachael's progress during Sunday school. She was in the C. C. Center in a wheelchair, undergoing physical therapy to strengthen her upper body. She was preparing to be able to lift herself up using the bars on the exercise walkway. The ultimate goal of the endeavor was to take a step or two.

This was going to be a long haul, even if it proved successful. At least her doctor was not giving up on her—considering her history of comebacks. She had great determination and courage, and she seemed to be less depressed than she had been—all positive attributes for recovery.

Francine brought her mother, Alice, to Sunday school, and everyone was happy to see her. She was the oldest living member at Hope Church. Her health had not been the best, but she still seemed sharp as a tack. During Sunday school, they asked her if she could still do the alphabet scriptures. She said, "I can. I go through them every time I can't sleep, and those occasions are more frequent these days."

The alphabet scriptures consisted of reciting a scripture that would begin with each letter of the alphabet from *A* to *Z*. So far, she was the only one in the class who had been able to master it every time. They loved to test her, and most of them had tried to learn all twenty-six but would miss one or two. It was a great exercise in memory control, and it also gave the scholar meaningful scriptures to recall in any circumstance.

She began, "Ask and it will be given to you. Blessed are the poor in spirit, for theirs is the kingdom of heaven. Come to me all you who are weary and burdened, and I will give you rest. Do to others as you would have others do to you, for this sums up the Law and the Prophets." She continued through to her usual ending, "Zippidy do dah and zing, zing, zing," which always got a good laugh from the others.

Of course, she wouldn't leave it there, so she said, "Zedekiah, son of Josiah, was made king of Judah by Nebuchadnezzar, king of Babylon."

Alice was a very bright woman, and it was such a blessing that she has kept her wits and her good humor throughout all her eighty-nine years.

Bea had asked, "Is everyone thinking about the October Fest? I've decided to make the peanut brittle again. How about you, Harriet? Yours is really good too."

"I'm not sure I'll be here. I may be traveling to Austria. If my sister can go, we'll be leaving in late September for a few weeks."

"Can you leave that puppy?" asked Anne.

"I don't know. He's such a sweetie, and we have a great relationship."

"Your son will look after him. You should live your life as you want," said Iola.

"We'll see."

"Iola, are you going to make some of those Monster Cookies?" asked Adele.

"No commitments at this time. We'll see how things go," said Iola.

Julia said she was going to make her orange cookies like she always did. "I'm really not in the mood to have all of that commotion throughout town again. I used to like it, but you can't even get through with all the people. When the children were little and could help, it was a lot different."

"None of the young people seem to be motivated either. We have quite a few living in the rentals, but they probably won't participate," said Laura. "Oh, they would if they could just put out a bunch of junk and call it 'treasurers,' but the borough commissioners said everything has to be home-baked or homemade. No more of those trashy items we had last year."

"Well, good!" said Anne. "Then if someone will share a porch with me, I'll make up some baby quilts. I've given away most of the full-sized quilts to my children and other family members. If I go to the trouble of making any more of those, they certainly won't be for a sale."

"You can come to my house," said Julia. "I'd welcome the company."

Adele had a great front porch, and Bea also had one. Laura would be there for sure. They could all find a good porch to sit on and sell their items if they really wanted to. Trouble was, no one was exactly enthusiastic to do it these days.

6

In the Fullness of Time

It was the first Sunday in August as Janine was getting dressed for church without an idea of where to go. "Which direction do you want to go this time?" she asked John.

He hesitated for a minute and said, "I was thinking of that church on the knoll of West Hope. It's the same denomination we've always known, and we might feel a bit more comfortable with the order of worship. What do you think?"

"I guess we might as well."

They drove up the little road leading to the church, and there were a good many cars on the upper grounds on a very nice, paved parking lot. They pulled in and wondered which door to enter. No one was around to ask; then a lady drove up, and they waited for her. She was dressed in a beautiful pink suit, had pretty white hair, and was very neat in appearance.

"Let's ask her," John said.

They got out of the car, and she looked their way. "Good morning," they said to the lady. "Are we late for church?"

"No, we're just on time."

"Do we go in this door then?" John asked.

"Yes, follow me." She seemed to be a bit shy and didn't offer her name.

They picked up a bulletin from the table in the narthex. The lady had disappeared, so they went over to the sanctuary doors and entered. The church had two aisles. They chose the left one. The back pew was empty, and it sat right in front of beautifully stained, open windows. They sat precisely as the service was beginning. The sanctuary was in the shape of a half circle—almost. They could see across the people on the opposite side pretty well. Most of the people were in the two-side sections, all facing the pulpit and the choir loft. There were fewer in the center.

Everyone looked so nice, dressed in his or her Sunday best. That was good. They had been in one or two churches where people came rather dressed down. Janine always said we should present ourselves respectably before the Lord in worship—clean and neat at the very least.

The worship bulletin followed the same worship pattern as they had become used to, and it was comforting.

Over in the far section, some were a-buzz about the couple that had just sat down.

Iola leaned over to Harriet, "Who are those who just came in?"

"I have no idea. I don't think I've ever seen them before."

Hmm . . . Somebody new over there! At least I don't know them, Bea was thinking.

The minister, Rev. Daniel Campbell, welcomed everyone and called for announcements. There were a few. Janine and

John had no idea who they were talking about, of course. But it was interesting in a way. The choir sang a nice introit and the service officially began with Reverend Campbell calling one and all with a scripture from 1 Chronicles 16:11-12:

> Seek the Lord and his strength;
> Seek his face evermore!
> Remember his marvelous works, which he has done,
> His wonders, and the judgments of his mouth.

Reverend Campbell was articulate and enjoyable to listen to, and Janine and John were attentively focused for the first time in a long time. When the minister announced the morning worship scripture, Janine turned to the Bible in the pew to read along.

Mathew 7, beginning with verse 7:

> Ask and it will be given to you; seek and you will find;
> Knock and the door will be opened to you. for
> everyone who asks receives; he who seeks finds;
> And to him who knocks, the door will be opened.
> Which of you, if his son asks for break, will give
> him a stone?
> Or if he asks for a fish, will give him a snake?
> If you, then, though you are evil, know how to give
> good gifts to your children,
> How much more will your Father in heaven give
> good gifts to those who ask him?

Janine had memorized this scripture and repeated it to herself quite often. Reverend Campbell certainly had a wonderful message based upon trusting that the Lord hears and answers prayers.

As Janine sat there feeling totally at ease with the service and the message, a gentle wind brushed across the back of her neck. The breeze got her attention while God gave her a message: "You are here."

She was nearly overcome with gladness, but she retained her composure. Attendance pads were passed along each pew. John signed for them and passed it to Janine. When she handed it over to the man seated on the other end of the pew, he smiled broadly, read their names, and signed it himself. As soon as the benediction was pronounced, that same man shook their hands and welcomed them to the church. John later said he had very big, strong hands and was probably a farmer.

A few of the members greeted them as they went toward the door. One was "Leola" or something like that. She was very friendly and invited them to come back. An elderly lady (she couldn't remember her name) also talked with them both and even asked where they lived. She seemed happy to hear that they were from McCade Road. Many of the members were standing around in clusters, seemingly not wanting to leave just yet.

Reverend Campbell shook their hands and asked their names. They told him they had recently moved into the area, and he said he hoped to see them again sometime. They left through the doors they had entered earlier. There were still a lot of cars on the parking lot. Apparently, no one was in a hurry to leave. They walked over to the car, got in, and Janine couldn't hold back the tears any longer. John didn't turn on the ignition immediately. He just turned and looked at her lovingly.

"John, it truly felt right. I think we should continue coming here. The breeze through the open window felt to me like God whispering, 'You are here.'"

"I know." He started the ignition, put the car into gear, and as they were going down the sloping drive, he said, "And you know what . . . You are here. You are in West Hope, the community you have said for years was calling you."

"John . . . you are right! Why oh why didn't I think of that before? I never ever made that connection."

"Looks like now you are going to get your wish and find out more about the people here after all." He smiled a smile that just wouldn't quit. She, on the other hand, could hardly see through her tears. She prayed silently, *Thank You, Lord. My joy is too much at this moment. You've given me something I never even requested. It was just a dream such as a child would have . . . wasn't it?*

John said, "Seek and you will find."

Two days later, they received a nice card from "Iola." *That was her name!* It said it was good having them worship at West Hope Church, and she hoped to see them again. "If you have any needs, please feel free to contact the minister, Reverend Campbell, at the church office."

7

A Day in the Life

Julia was calling Iola. "Did you get the names of the people who came on Sunday? You always seem to do that."

"I did. All I had to do was read the pew attendance book. I sent them a card. Their names are 'Stephens.'"

"Hmm . . . I don't think I know any Stephens. Do they live around here?"

"Not far. They are on McCade Road. I drove over that way yesterday just out of curiosity. I think they bought the Stafford house. Poor ol' Minnie. She's not doing well at all. I suppose Jake just couldn't keep up."

"Probably not . . . People come and people go. We'll see." Iola wished that were not true.

"It's so hot today. I wish it would rain and cool things down a bit."

"I know, but it would just add humidity and that could be worse. You could go sit on the porch. Maybe it's cooler outside."

"I tried that. It didn't help. And those noisy trucks spoil a good, relaxing sitting."

"Would you want to walk down to the store? I need some things and thought I'd put on my comfortable shoes and walk. I'll come by." Iola always enjoyed walking but not so much lately with her bunion.

"Okay. Better than just sittin' here, I suppose."

They lived just a few houses apart, though on most days, it could have been miles for all they saw of each other. Iola was there in no time. Julia picked up her purse and met her on the sidewalk.

"Do you think we'll ever get new sidewalks? I'm half afraid to walk on these stones." Julia remarked.

"What?"

"The sidewalks!" She looked straight at her, knowing she wasn't hearing her. "Do you think we'll ever get new ones?"

"New ones?"

"Yes!"

"Who would do it? The borough can't afford it, and the state wouldn't consider this their responsibility. I think each homeowner could contract a new sidewalk. Why don't you do that?"

"One short sidewalk won't make a difference at all."

"It might put the thought into another's mind and then another. Those things work sometimes." Iola was always figuring up solutions to problems.

"Yes, I suppose. But I'm not going to be the one to start it."

Although most people thought the sidewalks were quaint, they weren't. *Quaint is nice until someone falls!* Julia was thinking.

"When are you going to have your bunion removed?"

"What?"

Julia stopped and pointed to Iola's foot. "Your bunion. Are you going to have it removed?"

"Oh, I thought about it some more. I'm going to do it in January when I have nothing at all to do but sit inside."

"Makes sense."

They went into the store, which was air-conditioned and blessedly cool. There were a few other folks there—probably to cool off!

Hayden said, "Hello, ladies! Warm enough for you?"

"Hello, Mr. Carter. It certainly feels wonderful in here," said Iola. "How are you and Ms. Elda?"

"Oh, we're very fine, thank you. Yessiree. Very fine. Can I get you something?"

"Pardon me?" He found out suddenly that she did not have her hearing aid.

"We're fine." He spoke very clearly and cut it short.

"That's good!" she responded and wandered toward the canned goods.

"How 'bout you, Ms. Julia?"

"I'll just look around a bit," she said.

Julia decided she'd better get some Band-Aids. She didn't have any the other day when she cut her thumb. So she picked up a box of assorted sizes, ordered a few slices of Longhorn cheese, and bought a Milky Way candy bar. She was going to freeze it to eat later while watching the baseball game.

Julia walked over to the third aisle and found Iola, who was intently studying a box of something.

"What's that?" Julia asked.

"Now, just look at this! There are so many ingredients that you wouldn't even need any potatoes in the box. I can hardly pronounce all of these things, and they probably would not be good for you at all. I was going to buy a prepared scalloped-potato mixture, but I don't think I will. And the calories! Good heavens! I was going to try to eat more vegetables, but certainly not this."

"Why don't you buy a baking potato and just eat the whole thing? I do that sometimes."

"What?"

"Bake a potato!" She raised her voice. "Makes a meal," Julia offered.

"I couldn't eat an entire potato."

"You could too. And you could fix a salad. That would be lots of vegetables."

"Salads? Well, I don't actually like salads. My doctor would really like it if I would eat more salads, but I'm not ready to yet."

"Hmm . . . Did you ever try one of those frozen dinners?"

"Do you eat those? I do!" She really hadn't heard the question.

"Sometimes I cook up a big pot of soup or chili and have it all week."

She apparently understood her because she replied, "I like variety." She looked again at the box of scalloped potatoes and decided to go ahead and buy it.

"What did you buy?" Iola asked.

She showed her. "Oh, just a few slices of cheese and a candy bar."

Iola asked, "Are you going to watch the ball game on television tonight?"

"Yes," Julia answered. She was thinking, *I'm glad there's something on to watch. If I try to read, I just go to sleep.*

"I'll be watching too."

As they were checking out, Mr. Gordon came through the door, wiping the perspiration from his neck and brow. "G'day, me ladies!" he said. The ladies were always charmed by Mr. Gordon.

"And how're ye on this bonnie, bright day?" he asked.

The ladies responded with smiles and were suddenly charming too.

"Good day to you, Mr. Gordon," Julia said quite nicely.

Iola nodded her head as a fine English woman of the nineteenth century would do and said very properly, "Mr. Gordon, sir."

"Mr. Gordon, nice to see you. You surely are not out walking in this heat, sir?" asked Hayden.

"I am, at that. Exercise is goud fer the body and the soul anytime o'the year. However, I could use me self a good chilled glass o'yer fine lemonade, if you 'ave any t'day."

"That we do. Have yourself a seat and cool down. I'll go see about the drink for you."

The ladies left, bidding Mr. Gordon and Mr. Carter *adieu.*

"Do ye 'ave the *Daily*?" asked Mr. Gordon.

"Sure do, over there on the bench. Help yourself. Nothing good in the news these days though."

"'Ere's the truth if ever 'twas spoken. What's wrong with the world? I c'n tell ye what! 'Ere's people tha' need t'git 'emselves a wee neighborhood t'live in such as we 'ave 'ere and settle down to some goud, clean livin'."

"You have the answer! Yessiree! That's it . . . Just so's they don't all come here!"

Mr. Carter and Mr. Gordon always had fine conversations. They could settle the world's problems in a minute. Most of the men of the area could. Nothing was better than to have two or three of the gentlemen in at the same time discussing any given problem. They often did that.

"Tha' lemonade was on the spot! Well, off t'the brothy I go. We're 'avin' Cock-a-leekie soup. One o'me favorites."

"Very well, come see us again."

"That I will! G'day."

ᘀ ᘀ ᘀ

Rachael had just returned from physical therapy, quite pleased that she had completed her exercise for the first time. She was more determined now to get herself back on her feet. The one thing she wanted to do more than anything else was to be able to go back to her home and be on her own again. *It's no different than any of us would say. No one wants to be depending upon someone else. I always said that I would do everything I could to stay independent. If it means working hard at these exercises, then that's what I'm going to do.*

She had a terrific family. They were always coming to visit and bringing her reading materials. She's read anything from Shakespeare to government proclamations. She especially enjoyed reading novels that were issued in a series.

Another thing she enjoyed was making those crafts, and now she could once more. The center had arranged for her to go to a little room. They brought in her box of supplies so she could sit in her wheelchair and putter all she wanted to. The staff knew that it was as good as any therapy they could offer. She was making some interesting wreaths from honeysuckle vines. Albert cut some for her and soaked them. She had to work with them while they were still damp so that she could twist them around in a wreath shape. Albert helped her twist some of them the week prior, and now she was having a great time putting on some adornments in the way of flowers, greenery, etc. People looked in on her and enjoyed seeing what she would be doing next. It was always that way with her. It was one of the exercises that kept her going today.

ᐱᐱᐱ

Owen needed a special chair. He could have one delivered at the order of his doctor. He was not breathing as well as he should have been, and so he was going to attempt to get used to sleeping upright. The chair would be delivered to their new apartment, and thankfully, they found someone to take the other. The old one was a standard recliner and did not have the special features he now needed.

Anne had been busy that day. The neighbor came early to pick up Owen's old chair. He was doing fine sitting in hers for the time being. "Owen, are you comfortable?" she asked.

"Oh yes. This is fine. I can wait it out without any trouble. How about you?"

"Oh, I'm fine. After we're finished with the chair-moving process, I want to take out my embroidery piece again. I wondered if I would ever pick up that piece I started fifteen years ago, and yet I realize that it would be the perfect gift for Sharon's graduation. I was so pleased when I looked at it and found it still in good shape.

"I'm going to the kitchen and fix us some lunch. Is soup fine for today?"

"That good soup you made yesterday?"

"Yes."

"It's delicious. I'll look forward to it . . . Did you meet the new tenants?"

"Yes. They seem very nice. I hope we get to know them. It will be good to have someone else living next to us here in the building."

"I hope he plays checkers," Owen remarked.

She went into the kitchen and started lunch. She wasn't yet used to this small apartment. She had "worked her fingers to the bone," as Jenny had so aptly put it, in the big old farmhouse. It was truly getting too much for her to manage. This was better, but it was going to take time to adjust. *Life is full of changes and adjustments.* She'd seen a lot of them. *It's just harder when we get old. When we were young, I could just flit here and there. It didn't matter where we lived or how many children we were taking care of either . . . energy wanes. I want to face up to it but am not doing so well at it right now. By the time Owen and I get going in the morning and I leave for my walk, half of the day is done.*

Then he takes a nap, and I pick up a little sewing or whatever, and the other half of the day is gone. I don't want to complain to anyone, and I have no right to. I am thankful that we've lived this long. This is the part that comes with old age, I guess. I hope I don't have to give in to it.

8

Adjustments

Life *was* full of adjustments! Anne had certainly rediscovered it recently, although she had made many during her eighty-three years. She'll face this one just as she had with motherhood, retirement, and now a reduction in active participation. She didn't need to work so hard anyway, but she needed to be doing something that was interesting. Being the oldest member, she had considered not attending the homemakers group anymore because she decided that the younger members would enjoy the organization more with members of the same age. She had mentioned this to her friend, Jane, in her recent letter to her. She and Jane had met in college many years ago, and they had remained best friends.

A letter from Jane contained, among other things, a message that she hoped would help:

Anne, I thought for a while about your letter. I myself have struggled with those same thoughts. I wrote in my journal on January 22, 1994, the following:

The elderly sometimes find themselves believing that they are not wanted by a younger group, when the complete opposite is true and beneficial to all ages. The wisdom of those who have lived fuller lives, who have experienced more, who have learned the truth are desperately needed and should be obtainable by the young; while those who are younger will supply life's energies and vitality to those who, during the senior years, are in great need of such. It is the perfect balance.

Every progressive group should contain people of various ages so that the sought-after progress may be attained.

Please rethink your observation, Anne. I did and have been quite happy with my decision to remain with those friends.

I pray that you and Owen will continue in good health and that you will find your new home filled with the love of Christ.

Your "old" friend, Jane.

Anne received something valuable that day. It was a complete turnabout in her conception of herself and her worth. She would stay with the homemakers, and she would be more aware of her part within that group. Her good friend, Jane, who always had straightforward and wise perceptions about many things, once again was quite helpful to her.

ᕕᕕᕕ

Rachael's adjustments depended mainly upon her health and her healing. But would she be able to recover enough to live alone? If not, *could* she adjust? She would not even ask herself that question today. She *would* recover enough, and she knew that many prayers were still being sent on her behalf. She knew the Lord would see her through. She had confidence in the power of prayer . . . and why not? Who could question it? Every day is another day of striving toward her goal, and she would keep trying and trusting.

ᕕᕕᕕ

Julia was so lonely, and she didn't even care to adjust! *Life is no pleasure at all when you have no one to share it with. Even Jenny has moved away. It was better when she could come over, and we'd at least have things we enjoyed talking about together. We had been best friends for a good, long time.*

I wish I could think of something to do. I don't crochet anymore, even after getting my cataracts removed. I completely don't want to. What else can I do? I can't go out alone at night. I don't drive much out of the borough. I just sit and wait for Sunday usually. I'm going to be eighty-six years old soon . . . Is that good or bad?

♈♈♈

Adele knew how to make adjustments in her life. She had learned that her only hope was her trust in the Lord. These days were lonely, but she had the Lord to talk with. He had helped her adjust to her daughter's utterly debilitating injury and her husband's death. She held on then and she still held on today. Adele was an inspiration to many as she carried on with a smile and loving nature.

She counted her blessings and was thankful. This didn't erase her pain, loneliness, and heartbreaks, but her gratitude for God's gifts helped her to embrace an appreciative perspective. Her faith in a new life in eternity for her daughter and a reunion with her husband and all loved ones granted her hope and peace.

♈♈♈

"Lonely" was the worst word in the world for Bea. She was a people person if ever there was one and had always been an active individual. She was lighthearted and so much fun. Now she searched for something to do that could gather people together.

No one seems to be interested in doing anything. My friends have gotten old. I'm older than most of them, and I still feel young enough to do lots of things. It's frustrating!

There are enough of us in our Sunday school class to put our heads together and think of things we could do, but I sure don't see that happening.

I know that Iola loves to keep busy, but she is so serious about everything. I doubt if she could lighten up if she tried.

Anne has plenty to do. Owen keeps her company, and she sews and reads a lot. She likes that, I guess.

Laura has her husband, Ed, and he is not well at all. She needs to spend time with him.

Adele is my best friend. Sometimes we do sit and talk and play cards, but we don't do much else except go to church together.

Harriet is so involved in community affairs. My goodness! She must belong to a dozen different organizations. One day she had three meetings. Why would she do all of that? Maybe it's to fill time so she won't be lonely. That could be.

Julia never says much of anything. I think she looks forward to Sunday school, but I don't know if she does much more throughout the week. She's always been quiet.

Oh well. There's no sense in driving myself into total aggravation. She found no answer, so she turned on the TV and watched the news. She would never adjust to being old with nothing to do.

ᲚᲚᲚ

Janine Stephens saw her adjustment as joyful and exciting. The Lord had brought her into the Promised Land. *Everything is going to be wonderful,* she told herself nearly every minute. She still did not know what the Lord wanted of her here, but she trusted completely that she would know in God's time.

She told her daughters and her son all about the discovery of Hope Church. She couldn't stop marveling about the fact that it was in West Hope, the place she had felt tugging at her for years. Now, she was here, not by her own choice, but by the Lord's. This was a miracle in modern day. They say that miracles do not happen anymore, but no one could convince Janine of that.

9

"Amico Nuovo"

"Mother, my friend, Maggie Duncan, is a member of West Hope Church. I talked with her yesterday and discovered somehow that she actually saw you on Sunday. Are you going there again this week? If so, Maggie will probably introduce herself to you," Kathy said.

"She's a second grade teacher at my school and an especially nice person. You remember me telling you that I had Bible study with her?"

"Yes, I remember. I'll be there on Sunday. I hope she does let me know who she is. It will be nice to meet her."

The church was just about all Janine had on her mind right now. She could hardly wait for Sunday to come around again.

In the meantime, she had done a few other things. She telephoned the Detelle home, for one thing. Mrs. Geonna Detelle answered the phone and was very gracious. Janine said that she appreciated the visit from her son and her husband's parents and that she had a casserole dish that she would like to return at their convenience.

"Whenever it is convenient with *you* would be perfectly fine, Mrs. Stephens. Anthony's parents have spoken of you, and they have hoped that you would accept their invitation to come to our house. Please. When would you like to come?"

"Would tomorrow morning at ten thirty be all right?"

"Absolutely. It certainly would. We will be expecting you then."

Janine was a little nervous to go calling upon the neighbors in the big house; however, if Geonna was anything like Tony or Mario and Sophia, she would certainly enjoy meeting her.

She baked one of her special raisin/spice cakes to take to them. It seemed like the right thing to do.

John watched her go down the road and knew she was excitedly nervous. It was a pleasure to see Janine enjoying herself without the pressures as in the years past. She had been humming around all morning, fussing with icing on her special cake. She had a store-bought plate that would not need returned because she didn't want them to feel that this was going to be an unrelenting situation where each was now on the returning end—not that it would be a terrible situation at all.

She drove in through the beautiful pillars and up the curved-paved drive. It had paving of red bricks, about three feet wide on both sides of the drive. What an appealing look it presented, and standing on the outside of the curves were lampposts. *This must look just beautiful at night,* she thought.

The house was incredible. First thing she noticed were the beautiful windows. They were of grand designs and could have been imported. She wouldn't know! The front entrance did not have a porch but a few steps leading to a double door with beveled-glass windows. The brickwork on the entire structure was magnificent. She wasn't surprised about that because every Italian who could afford a brick home would want such as this. The bricks in various places were appointed in patterns. She was so entranced with the house, she almost forgot to get out of the car!

Sophia and Mario stood in the open door, all smiles! They stepped forward to extend to her their sincere welcome.

Janine walked up with her little cake in hand and was so happy to be there. It was a moment that she accepted as a gift. She felt that she would be a friend with these two and that it was not an accident.

Mario at once took her hand in both of his to indicate that he was happy to have her there. Sophia embraced her! "Welcome, *il mio amico nuovo*." How wonderful! Janine felt welcomed all right as she returned the embrace.

"Come in. Come in!" Mario gestured toward the door.

She was wondering if Geonna was home but didn't say anything. It was especially nice that these two whom she had already met came to the door themselves. They entered into a totally different world: chandeliers, marble floors, beautiful paintings, and an abundance of light and color. She almost lost her ability to speak but composed herself immediately.

"Come. We will sit-a here," Sophia said. Janine handed her the cake, and she placed it on the hall table as they entered the gorgeous living room with beautiful floral-patterned chairs and settees. The fabrics were exquisite. She decided she would not look around anymore. After all, her visit was with these beautiful, dear people. *Who cares where they live?*

"You like-a da rigitone?"

"It was delicious! Thank you so much."

Sophia and Mario beamed.

"You happy where you live-a now?" Sophia asked.

"I am *very* happy. I came from Innesport where I had lived most of my life. This is a big change for me, moving from the city to the country . . . And it's so quiet out here. I like it."

"We know about changing too. We come from another country! But we are very happy to be in America with our son and Geonna and the children. They have done everything for us. Our homeland is our homeland. We will always love Italy, but to be with Anthony and his family and many new friends here in America is much-a better for us." Mario expressed himself passionately as she would have expected.

"Have you ever returned to Italy for a visit?"

"Many, many times. Anthony . . . He takes us. We see other people we know and other family people too. We fly. We enjoy."

"I hope that someday I will travel to Italy. It is a place I have always wanted to go, but for now, I am very happy to be where I am!"

Geonna came into the room. No! Geonna *entered* the room with grace and elegance. She was slender and beautiful with a sincere smile. She exuded sophistication, rarely seen throughout the region.

She moved swiftly to Janine and held out her hand to her in welcome.

"Janine, we have already met on the telephone. It's good to have you here with us now," she said.

Janine stood to receive the welcome and thanked her. Geonna sat down near to her, and they began a discussion of small things. They both seemed to be enjoying the acquaintance time. They spoke of their children mainly, which is what mothers do.

Geonna stood and invited Janine into her kitchen. This was the highest invitation from any Italian host. Janine was delighted. They all went into a kitchen that was directly out of *House Beautiful*, or some such magazine.

Geonna said that Sophia enjoyed the kitchen, and she was so happy to have her here to teach her all the wonderful ways of cooking that she knew. Sophia was a very good cook, and her daughter-in-law hoped that someday she would receive the compliment of cooking just like her amazing teacher.

This is a wonderful arrangement. Each is happy with her position in the family.

They sat at a table adorned with flowers and beautiful placemats and had a cup of coffee together. She was offered a piece of Sophia's bread, and even though she had told herself she would pass on any food today, she took it and was glad she did.

It was a good visit. Janine was happy to have made this connection. She had hoped that they would continue forward with being neighborly. She left with a glowing sense that her life had just been brightened. *How long has it been since I actually met someone I had never known?* She was exploding with energy and vigor—a rejuvenation of sorts.

10

The First Day of the Week

Janine couldn't sleep on Saturday night. She finally got up at five o'clock, made coffee, read her Bible, and prayed. Suddenly, she heard the birds singing and realized that it was dawn. She broke away from her quiet moments, opened up the sliding doors on the kitchen, and slipped outside in her nightgown and robe.

What a beautiful morning. I'm glad I didn't miss this! The sun was, at that very moment, coming up over the horizon—big, bright, and beautiful. *When have I seen a sunrise?* She asked herself. The houses and buildings of the city had kept her from this heavenly experience too long! The few scattered clouds were absorbing the golden glow of the sun and reflecting the splendor across the sky. *Exactly as we absorb and reflect the glow of the Son of God.*

How many mornings had she wasted behind drawn blinds, refusing to let the light shine in? From now on, she would get out of bed early, spend more time with the Lord, and receive an early blessing of the Son and the gift of the sun.

She was so excited and grateful to be discovering yet another blessing from the Lord. *I had no idea of the many, many blessings. Doesn't the psalmist say, there are too many to grasp? There are!*

She had to pull herself away and go on inside. She took a shower and began to fix breakfast as John came in, rubbing his eyes.

"Hey! What time did you get up?"

"Before sunrise, which gave me the opportunity to go out on the deck and witness it this morning. It was spectacular! I'm planning to do that again tomorrow. What a way to start the day!"

"Good for you! Are you cooking breakfast? This is interesting. You who would rather have a banana and go on?"

"I had time. I have no reason to rush. I'll not be playing the organ or be responsible for anything today . . . and I'm feeling hungry from being up a while. Why don't you go freshen up and we'll sit down together to pancakes and eggs?"

"Mmm, mmm! That sounds good. I'll be right back."

They talked and talked. How can two people who see each other most of every day find so much to talk about? But they did most of the time. It was a nice, slow-paced breakfast and very enjoyable for both of them.

$$\gamma \gamma \gamma$$

They knew which door to walk through at Hope Church this time, so that made them feel better and somewhat familiar with the church. They no sooner got inside when Mr. Kirkland welcomed them and handed them bulletins. He said he was happy to see them and seemed to mean it.

They ambled on to the pew they had last week and sat down. The window was once again open. Apparently, the church had no air-conditioning, or perhaps they didn't use it unless it was a must. This church seemed to be populated with Scottish names, meaning one big thing: don't spend what you don't have to!

John smiled at that thought. *Let's see, the elders have names of Kirkland, Severight, Davidson, and Dawson. Yep! There are probably more folks who are not on this list who are of the same heritage. We should fit in pretty well.*

Maggie was right in front of them! Of course, they didn't know last week that she was Kathy's friend. Following them into the sanctuary, she had addressed them both and introduced herself. She was a woman of about forty, tall and strong looking. She was pleasantly eager to bid them welcome and tell them how much she enjoyed her relationship with Kathy. Her husband sat down as soon as he was introduced. He leafed through his bulletin and obviously was not as outgoing as his wife, which was usually the case in most families.

Janine sat down too because the organist had just walked in and the music was beginning. *Were these people actually going to listen to the prelude?* Some did. Not all . . . but at least some did. She was very interested in—*What's her name? Oh, here it is . . . Francine Simmons. That name sounds familiar. I don't believe I know her though.*

Janine enjoyed Francine's rendition of a favorite hymn, "It Is Well with My Soul," and decided to concentrate on her gladness and appreciation. That was easy!

The minister and the choir came down the aisle. There weren't many—eight or nine—and had sounded adequate last week. They had no director, but apparently, Francine did it all, and they just followed her from the organ bench. It was not the best of situations, but sometimes we do what we can. It was not a big church after all, and at least they were here doing the Lord's work.

The call to worship was from Psalm 24:1-4:

> The earth is the Lord's, and everything in it:
> the world, and all who live in it:
> for He founded it upon the waters.
>
> Who may ascend the hill of the Lord?
> Who may stand in His holy place?
>
> He who has clean hands and a pure heart,
> who does not lift up his soul to an idol
> or swear by what is false.

The first hymn was "How Great Thou Art." They stood, and she enjoyed singing without playing for a change, especially after the Sonrise Experience.

There's the lady a couple of pews down who had that nice pink suit on last week and came into the church the same time we did. Over there on the other side is that "Iola" lady who sent us the card. I want to be sure to thank her.

The minister had announced that the newsletters were ready for pickup in the narthex and there were extra copies for guests. *That is something I don't want to forget. It should be interesting.*

The service continued, and Janine and John enjoyed it as much as last week. They stood for the benediction, and Mr. MacMillan, who was there last week, introduced himself by name this time. Maggie turned around and greeted them again, and Mrs. Iola MacCowan rushed over to greet them.

"Mrs. MacCowan, thank you for the nice note. We really appreciated it."

"You're welcome. It's good to see you here again this Sunday. Will you be coming back?"

"We do plan to."

She was obviously very happy to hear that and went on over to the other section from which she had come. She immediately engaged in conversation with the others over there.

As the Stephenses were walking on toward the minister, Mr. MacMillan handed them one of the newsletters. They thanked him and tucked it away for later.

"They said they plan to return next Sunday," Iola told the ladies gathered together on the other side. Julia and Jenny, who had sat on the left side as usual, had moved to the other side to talk with their friends.

"Who?" asked Julia.

"That new couple sitting behind you. I don't suppose you have eyes in the back of your head though. We need more people here."

"I saw them last week," said Jenny. "I didn't notice this morning."

"Anybody going to lunch?" asked Julia.

Most were, so they made their way to the parking lot to load up.

A few more people greeted John and Janine; then they shook hands with the pastor and went outside. It was a beautiful day. *Just look at that stunning farm down there. I didn't notice it last week, but I had other things on my mind,* thought Janine.

"John, did you see the farm?" he said he did as he looked over her shoulder. "Pretty nice, huh?"

She got in the car, and they drove out of town and on home.

ᎽᎽᎽ

The ladies went to lunch and sat at their usual table, tucked in the corner away from most of the others.

"Did you see here in the newsletter that the softball game is next week?" asked Bea.

"I saw it. I don't know if I'm going or not," said Julia.

"Why wouldn't you? You like baseball, and most of the church members will be going. What do you want to do? Sit all alone in your house?" asked Bea.

"Well, it's going to be hot in the afternoon sun," said Julia.

"So what? You could wear a hat . . . And if you aren't going to play in the game, you can sit on the shaded bleachers," Bea said.

"Play? Heaven forbid. I am certainly not going to play," said Julia.

"Where'd you get that idea, Bea? The game is for kids and the men," said Jenny.

"Who says?" Bea responded.

"Wait a minute now. Please tell me you aren't really thinking of getting out there and playing," said Iola.

"I *am* going to play. I bought me a new ball cap, and my old glove is fine, and I'm playing! I think I'll volunteer to pitch."

They were aghast. It was getting worse every minute!

Adele was listening while laughing inside. She knew this was coming after their conversation sometime back. The reaction was hilarious, and the funniest thing was that Bea was absolutely serious.

"Bea, for heaven's sake, you are going to get yourself injured or fall or something and then you'll be laid up. It's not worth it. You're too old." Iola just told her the way it was.

"Hey! If you don't want to play, then just don't play." She couldn't believe there would be such fuss over her wanting to participate in something that she would enjoy. *What fuddy-duddies!*

"I can't believe you all are so narrow minded. A person has a right to have a little fun. I don't care how old I am. I feel good enough to do it, and I'm gonna do it . . . Now, let's order."

"Well, you just go ahead if that's what you want. But don't forget . . . we told you so," Iola spoke up for herself and the others.

ʏʏʏ

"Hmm, says here that the social committee of Hope Church is sponsoring a softball game at the community park next Sunday. 'Come on down and enjoy the fun. Teams will be chosen by numbers. During and after the game, there will be free hot dogs, hamburgers, and cool drinks.' Wanna go?" John read.

"I don't know. We don't know anybody yet. Maybe next year. I didn't even know there was a park around, did you?"

"We could find out easily enough. Mr. MacMillan would tell us, or anybody else, I should think. I don't know, Janine, this would be an opportunity to observe some of the members in a fun and informal situation. It might be worth our while, and it might also be fun for us. Think about it. I'll leave the newsletter here for you to read. There are some interesting articles."

Janine was a bit preoccupied with trying to locate some important papers she had lost during the move. It was always something.

"Hello," John answered the telephone. "Hey! Honey, it's Harry! How're ya doin'? You're what? . . . How'd you get that idea? . . . Huh! . . . That sounds like something you'd really enjoy, and something only an engineer could construct . . . What? Did you have any help? Ha ha ha . . . Then, what?"

"John, what on earth?" He waved her off.

She walked out of the room so that Harry could finish his one-sided conversation with his father. *Honestly, those two. When they were into it, forget trying to break in.*

She went on into the so-called computer room that was full of boxes at this point. She guessed that the file she was looking for was in there. She began going through some and then decided that the room should be tackled for organization. Of course! She got lost in her attempt, and before she knew it, nearly an hour has passed.

Was John still on the phone?

She went back to the kitchen, and he was saying, "Here's your mother. She'll want to say 'Hi.'"

So now, I'm going to get to say "Hi" while he has said volumes.

"Hello, sweetheart."

"How's my mom?"

"Wonderful—really wonderful."

"Dad tells me you found the answer to your prayer."

"I did! Isn't that just the greatest thing? Whenever I think about how awesome that is, I am overwhelmed. Mostly, I find it incredible that God can pay that much attention to me when there are so many other prayers going to Him and so many more important things for Him to be thinking about."

"'His eye is on the sparrow,' you know."

Ha! He's following in his father's footsteps with a quote! That's fine with me.

"Hey! You always taught us to believe and have faith. Now you have shown us *how* to believe and have faith. Good lessons, Mom. I'm really looking forward to regular updates on this new path you are taking. I hope it's not the speed path you were on before. It is an astounding story, Mom. This will be one for the books!"

"What books?"

"Well, for years, you have told us you wanted to write. You don't want to keep this to yourself, do you?"

"Now, Harry. I'm not going to write a book! It's only been a dream. Look at how long I've talked about it. Did I ever give any indication I would actually do it? I don't think I ever really will."

"Well, don't give up on your dreams, Mom. They *can* come true!"

"How's the family? Let me talk with the boys."

"Okay. They're just itching to speak to you."

As usual, they were lined up, and each, in turn, told Janine whatever was on his mind. It was always great no matter what they had to say, be it something about school, bugs, or storms. She could listen to those dear stories forever.

"Well, you got an earful this time, didn't you?"

"I sure did, Harry. What were you and your father talking about that engrossed him so much—or should I just ask him?"

"Oh, he'd better tell you. I have to get going here. We have some fun things planned for this afternoon, and all of us are ready and rarin' to go. I'll call next week."

"Okay, honey. Tell Rhonda we love her. Love you too."

"I love *you*, Mom. Bye."

She hung up the phone and stared into space for a while, not wanting to release the voices. If someone had asked her years ago if she could live without her family near her, she would have said "No! Never!" But somehow, she had come to accept the fact that a "man must leave his mother" and go lead his own life. Harry seemed happy enough. She forgot to ask him if he would get any time to come home this year. "Home"? *There's an interesting word. Where is "home"?*

On second thought, she would not be asking him that question.

One of the most distressing things Harry had ever said to her was on the telephone a year after he had ventured out on his own. He wasn't married at the time but had settled out there with a good job in Oklahoma. He found it to be the right place for him, and one evening as he and his mother were in conversation, she asked, "When will you be home?"

His response was, "I *am* home, Mom."

The sudden realization of what that actually meant cut her through like a knife. Up to that point, she had hoped that he would return or, at the very least, always consider his parents' home as "home." The fact that it wasn't true anymore was a crushing blow.

She got over it all, as mothers must, was thankful for his love and his goodness, and prayed for him to be happy. That was always the major concern of a mother. *We will never lose our children if we don't cling too tightly.* She learned that valuable lesson, and they—and she—were all doing well.

11

Take Me Out to the Ball Game

Most of the people at Hope Church were dressed for the softball game when they came to church Sunday morning. Of course, Janine and John didn't think about doing that. That was okay. If they were going to go to the park (wherever it was), they could just slip on home and change without losing too much time.

There was excitement in the air all through the service. Accordingly, the minister had prepared a praise service for the morning, which was not so restricted. Janine didn't like "messing around" with the order of worship normally but had to admit that she enjoyed it today. More contemporary music was used, which she did not know, but liked them and felt the music added considerably to the style of the service. *I hope they don't do this too often.*

They arrived early, and when Mr. MacMillan sat down, they had a few minutes to speak to him. Mr. MacMillan spoke first. "Please call me Raymond. My wife's name is Lucy, and she sings in the choir. She's a soprano in the second row. We have a dairy farm out a ways. My mother was a Croft. The family's been here for generations."

"Oh, that's nice," said Janine. "This is John and I am Janine. We just moved in to the area in June. Our family is grown, so we're by ourselves now. We hope to get to know all of you better in time. This is a real nice church."

"Thank you. I think so. Of course, I wouldn't know any other. I was baptized here as a baby and hope to be buried here when I die. I have nothing to compare this church to actually. I have gotten acquainted with some of the folks from other churches around as we have gatherings together at times, but I'm perfectly satisfied with where I am right now. Are you going to the softball game today?"

John spoke up, "We didn't plan on it."

"I think it would be a good thing, especially if you are going to be a regular here. You would have a chance to get around and talk to people. Lucy and I would be happy to accompany you to the park and sit with you in the bleachers. Unless, of course, you want to play ball."

"Good heavens, no. I don't think I'll do that this time. Thank you for your offer. What do you say, Janine?"

"I think that's very nice of you, Mr. Raymond, you say?" He nodded. "Well, we obviously are not dressed for the occasion, but we could meet you at the park."

"Fine. Fine. We'd be most proud to have you join us."

John had to ask, "Where is the park, Raymond?"

"Oh, sorry, I just assumed . . . You go to the end of the borough that way and come to Mercy Street on the left. Just turn there and you'll see the park right quick."

"Then so it is. We'll see you there later, and thank you very much for your invitation. We do appreciate it," John said.

The prelude was beginning, and it was an old-fashioned tune with a gospel swing. *Good for you, Francine. You certainly are right on,* thought Janine. She wore a smile all through the morning.

At the end of the service, Raymond introduced them to a few of the others sitting near. Francine came down the aisle and practically bumped into Janine. "Oh, excuse me. I shouldn't be in such a hurry. Sorry."

"That's fine. I enjoyed your music, even though I really didn't know many of the songs. Do you use contemporary songs often?"

"Oh goodness, no! This congregation would probably tar and feather me if I tried that more than once in a blue moon. They like the hymns that they were brought up with mostly, but they humor me now and then. I don't know how I caught on to some of these new ones myself since I am such a 'died in the wood,' as they say.

"Anyway, my name's Francine Simmons. It's very nice having you worship with us."

"I'm Janine and this is my husband, John. Let me introduce him to you."

After a few words, the Simmonses were scampering for the door, and Janine said to John, "Francine and Lawrence Simmons. Now do you remember?"

He scratched his head, blinked a few times, and the light turned on inside of his head. "The sign . . . They were the bride and groom here that day."

Janine giggled and nodded. They were enjoying this recollection and putting it all together with the actual people. The newly married couple was not at all what they expected. *One never knows . . . Very interesting!*

Maggie Duncan finally got through to speak to the Stephenses. "Hello. I'm so glad to see you again. You might try to get that daughter of yours to come with you some Sunday. I've invited her, but I certainly wouldn't want to take her away from her own church. Are you going to the ball game?"

"I guess so."

"Good, then we'll see you later. I have to go locate my husband and get going. See you at the park."

"Okay!"

The church emptied much faster than usual because they all had somewhere to go. Cars were filling up and moving out. "Head 'em up. Move 'em out," John said.

They felt lighthearted after the friendliness and joviality of the morning. They hurried home, jumped into blue jeans, and were on their way to the ballpark. Janine tried to recall if she had ever felt so good about participating in a church event before. She couldn't. Her church in the city didn't plan events such as these.

ᐱ ᐱ ᐱ

The park was easy to find. *How could anyone get lost in this little community anyway?* There were maybe sixty-five to seventy-five people there. Two teams were being chosen by numbers. Someone saw the Stephenses coming in and yelled, "Hi. Come on over and get on a team!"

Well, Janine was not going to do it. No way! John had said he wasn't going to either, but that didn't last. He went right over and was immediately placed on a team. He had no glove, no hat, or anything. Now what?

Oh, there were Raymond MacMillan and his wife, Lucy, coming toward her. Thank goodness. John had casually as anything deserted her!

"Mrs. Stephens, I'd like for you to meet my wife, Lucy."

"Oh, please call me Janine. How do you do, Lucy? Your husband has been very gracious to invite us here today."

"Are you going to play ball?" Raymond asked.

"No. I'm going to watch. How about you?"

"No. No . . . We'll just be cheerleaders. Come on and join us. Would you like a refreshing, cool drink first?"

Since they both were carrying one, she said she would, and they walked over to the table with the big self-serve thermoses and Styrofoam glasses and helped herself. They then climbed up onto the bleacher.

Lucy and Raymond did their best to introduce her around. She would never remember names but would likely remember their faces. That was fine. No one expected her to remember so soon.

Up on top was Maggie, waving to her. Over on the bottom and to the left were some of the older-looking ladies. She remembered Iola but hadn't really met the others.

Adele was there to support Bea in whatever she decided to do. She was sure she was going to play because she had her ball cap on and that funny T-shirt with a cartoon drawing of an off-balance pitcher that looked like a Norman Rockwell drawing. Bea was over, talking with the group gathered around home plate.

Iola and Harriet were there, fussing and fuming about Bea's efforts to hurt herself. None of the others in the class wanted to sit in the sunshine and heat, so they stayed at home.

"Oh, look! There's little Jimmie Adams. He'll want to play ball, but he and his family never come to church," said Iola.

"I say let him play. What a shame! His parents could care less about him," said Adele. "Sometimes I see him out on the sidewalks late at night. They probably don't know where he is."

"I know. They tell me he does all right in school when he's there."

"Look, they're getting ready to side up. Is that Beatrice Roberts going to the mound?" Lucy asked.

Harriet turned around and said it was.

There was almost a gasp. Everyone was thinking that Bea was old and was going to get hurt out there. They were concerned that the ball might come straight at her. There wasn't a whole lot of cheering going on because the crowd was holding its breath.

First at bat was little Jimmie, the leadoff batter. The preacher was the coach of that team. He knew the boy needed to be there.

Bea was winding up. Some wondered if she would throw her shoulder out of its socket. And the pitch—she actually got it to the plate, and Jimmie swung and missed.

The ball was thrown to Bea who caught it! She wound up again, looking at little Jimmie with beady eyes. Jimmie tried to loosen up, but she was intimidating him. Someone yelled, "Come on, Jimmie. Hit that ball!"

The pitch! Right across the plate and Jimmie hit it! The fans stood up and cheered for him. The ball was a ground ball right past the pitcher. Jimmie was on base. John was in the outfield, out of harm's way. *Good,* Janine thought.

Up next was a big man, perhaps about forty years old. He used his position to sneer at the pitcher. (All in good jest, of course.) She set those beady eyes again. The fans separated—half were cheering on the batter and the others were cheering for Bea. In truth, *everyone* wanted Bea to do well. Strike!

She caught the ball coming back to her from the catcher and then looked over at little Jimmie threateningly. He practically hugged the base. She stared down the batter, wound up, and let the ball go. The batter swung at the ball and missed. The ball went sailing up in the air over the catcher's head. It seemed Bea had gotten too enthusiastic. Everyone was cheering little

Jimmie to run. He ran to second base and was thrilled beyond measure.

Bea got the ball again, turned to Jimmie, and stared at him. The crowd was getting amused at Bea as she was portraying a tough guy for the fun of it and acting the part very well.

The batter whacked the next pitch, and it went sailing right at John!

"Get it, John!" Janine yelled. She had gotten caught up in the action. John had no glove of his own and had borrowed one that certainly didn't fit. As he reached for the ball, he missed it completely! He would not have caught that ball if he had on a $500 made-to-fit glove.

Janine hid her face. John ran after the ball. By the time he found it in the grass and picked it up and threw it as far as he could, both runners had scored.

What fun! Janine had never in her life enjoyed anything so much. *And that pitcher! What a character!*

Bea struck out the next batter, and the next one flied to the second baseman. One more out to go.

Bea was markedly wearing down, so the next batter, a young woman, took sympathy on her without her knowing it and missed the pitch. She missed the next one and the next. The inning was over. Bea had her fifteen minutes of fame, and someone else would get the opportunity to pitch an inning when it came up again. She was so tickled with herself for getting in there and doing it. One and all stood and someone started a cheer for Bea in the bleachers, and it continued until she came over and sat down with them.

Janine had never participated in anything like this—old and young together, having a great time—all members of the same "family."

John came over with a glass of lemonade and sat a minute or two. He and Janine got a good laugh out of his calamity in the last inning. He thought he might have to go to bat, so he went over to the dugout and put himself in the lineup. It was good that he was being a sport about it all, and everybody liked him for it.

Bea sat down with the cheerleaders who were all congratulating her. Some asked her if she felt okay. She felt *more* than okay really. She was having a great time. No one was surprised at anything Bea might do, except Janine, who was positively charmed by her. *Not many of her age would ever attempt such a thing. She must be a lot of fun to have around,* Janine thought.

Those not at bat or in the field were having hot dogs, as were the cheerleaders. *Mmm!* They were the best hot dogs Janine had ever tasted. *Is it the brand or do hot dogs always taste like this at a ball game?*

Who is that? It looks like Tony Detelle. I didn't know they were members of Hope Church. She asked Lucy, who said he wasn't a member but attended the youth meetings with his friends of the church. He was Catholic.

John's team (well, not *John's*) was now up at bat, and Tony was the leadoff batter. It didn't take long for him to hit one out of the park. There was another unified cheer by the cheerleaders.

Eight batters later and, finally, John came to the plate. He looked pretty good, and Janine hoped he didn't fan that bat around and get struck out.

The bases were loaded, and John was glaring down the poor fellow trying to pitch. He sent a pretty nice pitch over the plate. John let it go by. Strike!

Well, he was getting serious now, loosening up and preparing to really whack the ball. While he was messing around, preparing himself, the ball came whizzing right by. Now, that does it. He was doing a good job of entertaining the crowd. Janine had never really seen this side of him. He had apparently learned some points or two from the others.

The pitch! Ball!

The windup and the pitch . . . *Crack!* The bat broke! He'd have to hurry to get to first base, and here came the runner into home! John turned slightly to see if the runner had scored and lost his balance and down he went—smack on his stomach!

Janine was on her feet, afraid that he had hurt himself . . . No. He was back on his feet, running to beat the pitch to first base. The cheering was deafening. He ran as fast as he could, which unfortunately wasn't good enough and was out at first.

The crowd cheered for him as he brushed himself off and came over to the stands. He was holding out both hands and shrugging his shoulders, indicating, at least he tried. In doing so, he had missed a catch in the outfield, broken a bat, fallen down, was put out at first base, and gained the respect of everyone for his noble sportsmanship.

The game was over after four innings, which went quickly after the first inning, at which time the score had been 12-2. The score tightened up a bit at one point, but really, no one cared. Strikes or balls, runs or outs, made no difference. What mattered was the fellowship.

Lucy and Raymond did their best to introduce John and Janine around. The church members were warm and friendly toward them, and the day ended well as the crowd dispersed to go their separate ways.

The Stephenses went home, showered, rested, and felt great satisfaction in their day. The future was looking bright. *Thank You, Lord, for laughter and a really good time.*

Bea said before collapsing on the sofa, *Thank You, Lord, for laughter and a really good time, and for holding me up too.*

12

The Morning Celebration

It was another beautiful morning. Janine was up before sunrise again, made herself some coffee, and sat at the kitchen table with her Bible.

She opened to Psalm 24:1-6 as the pastor had read two Sundays ago.

> The earth is the LORD's, and everything in it, the world, and all who live in it.
>
> For he founded it upon the seas and established it upon the waters.
>
> Who may ascend the hill of the Lord?
>
> Who may stand in his holy place?
>
> He who has clean hands and a pure heart, who does not lift up his soul to an idol or swear by what is false.
>
> He will receive blessing from the LORD and vindication from God his Savior.
>
> Such is the generation of those who seek him, who seek your face,
>
> O God of Jacob.

Janine walked out on the deck. There was the slightest indication that the darkness would soon be completely gone. *The earth is the Lord's.* He will cause the sun to break forth and cover the earth, and she would wait and watch, leaning over the railing. *We still should get some chairs for out here.*

The birds began to sing. The volume increased as other birds joined in the chorus. She even heard a rooster in the distance. The light was coming! *What a process!* From pale softness of no color to a turning of soft pink that became more vibrant across the expanse of the sky in various tones of color. The birds were cheering and calling to one another in celebration. She was as excited as they were as she caught the very edge of the sun making an appearance.

In moments, it was up, and the earth was covered with light. After she said her morning prayers of thanksgiving and praise, she went back inside the house.

13

My Aching Back!

She thought she heard John rustling about and then saw him as well. He was slightly bent over and holding his back.

"Honey, what's wrong?"

"Oh! Oh! My back hurts! I guess it's from the fall yesterday!"

"Uh-oh! Does it ache or pain?"

He looked at her with a frown. "It hurts!"

"I know, but if it's pain, it could mean a pinched nerve or a disk problem, but if it's an ache, it could be muscle."

"Well, thank you very much for your quick diagnosis, Dr. Stephens."

"John, stop that. I'm trying to be helpful."

"Well, I don't know if it is aching or paining. I'd better call Dr. Lanza."

"Good idea. Do you want me to do it?"

"Okay. He won't be in yet, I don't suppose. I'll leave a message."

"Is that fresh coffee?"

"It was. It should be all right. I'll pour you a cup. Sit down, honey."

He moaned his way to a chair and inched his way into it, stiffened his back and held it.

"I'm not sure what to do for you right now. Ice for pain and heat for aches."

"Janine! For heaven's sake! When did you get into all of this?"

"All of what?"

"This 'voodoo' medicinal observation."

"Oh my, John." She was practically splitting her sides laughing at that. "Voodoo?" she asked.

"No, sorry. Not 'voodoo' . . . Shaman."

"Well, if that doesn't beat all." She laughed some more. "Well, if I am a shaman, I'd better get to the work of curing you . . . Bend over."

"What?"

"I'm going to apply some pressure and discover the center of the pain and then I'm going to take both fists and push it out of you."

"Janine?"

"Dr. Shaman please."

"That's enough!" He stood up and moved away from her, obviously not entirely trusting her at the moment. He wasn't in such a good position to defend himself.

"Oh, John, I was just having fun."

"Well, it doesn't seem like much fun to me."

"Okay. Okay. I'm sorry. I'll call Dr. Lanza and confer with him before prescribing any cures for you today."

She really was concerned about him but had such lightheartedness about her she became a little silly. *Get serious, Janine. He does hurt.*

She finally connected with the doctor's office and made a ten o'clock appointment for him. They had plenty of time.

ΥΥΥ

Beatrice had driven herself and Adele home after the ball game. She was as happy as a lark. Adele was happy for her too. She asked Bea if she thought she was going to be all right.

"I am all right. I had a real good time today. Hey! I'll see ya soon."

Adele got out of the car, and Bea went home. She went in through the garage door to the house, turned on a few lights, and looked at herself in the mirror. *I'm a mess. I have dirt on my face, and look at my crummy hair. I'm gonna have to take a shower. That's for sure!*

She took her shower right away and realized that she was pretty well tired out. She'd just jump into her pajamas and be ready for bed whenever she felt like it. She sat in front of the television but kept falling asleep. Rather than sleep uncomfortably there, she went on to bed. It was only nine o'clock.

At six o'clock the next morning, she awakened from a deep sleep and had to rush to the bathroom. She made it, but just barely, as she was stiff in the joints come morning.

She walked into the kitchen and realized when she reached for the teapot that her shoulder really hurt. *Yep! Sure doesn't surprise me. I haven't used those muscles for a coon's age. Uhgghh! I can hardly move my arm. I'll get some of that arthritis cream, rub it in, and take some ibuprofen. The aching is just a reminder of the good time I had yesterday. I don't care if I hurt. I've had lots of hurts in my lifetime.*

ᎶᎶᎶ

Alice Cook answered the telephone. Her daughter, Francine, was on the line. "Well, good morning. How are you today?"

"I'm fine, Mother. How are you?"

"No problems. Did you go to the ball game yesterday?"

"We did and had a really fun day of it. You should have seen Beatrice Roberts. She came to the game prepared to participate, and so they let her pitch the first inning."

"Good grief! What was she thinking?"

"You know Bea. She loves a good time. She just wanted to have fun, and it looks like she did."

"I hope she didn't get hurt or anything."

"No. She seemed fine to me."

"Well, good for her! Could she actually pitch the ball to home plate?"

"She did. I'll bet she's hurting this morning."

"She most likely is."

"We have a new couple in church. I think they've been there maybe two or three times. The name is Stephens. His name is John. I forget hers, but they may be in their late fifties or sixties. Nice-looking couple and I think they actually will stay."

"That's great news. I hope they do."

"Me too. I have no idea if they are retired or what their interests are, but they came to the game yesterday, and the man played ball and had a really good time. He seemed like such a good sport and very likeable."

Telephones were buzzing all around West Hope today. Julia called Jenny.

"Well, I guess we missed it yesterday."

"Missed what?"

"The ball game. I got brought up to date from Iola last night."

"Did Bea play ball?"

"She sure did. She pitched."

"Glory be! When is she going to stop taking such chances with her health?"

"I guess she did fine and was none the worse for doing it. I'm glad, but I'll tell you, you never know about her."

"Well, we all enjoy doing different things, I guess. As for me, I never did play ball. I haven't done much that would be classified as risky in my life that I know of. But then, I never really wanted to. We're all made differently, no matter what Thomas Jefferson proclaimed. Even the Bible says we each have different gifts."

"That's the truth. I don't want to criticize anybody. It's probably a good thing that we aren't all the same, or else, life would be pretty darned boring, don't you think?"

"Yes, I do. What are you doing today?" Jenny asked.

"There's nothing to do really. The cleaning lady might get here this week. The house could use some freshening. I've been kind of watching for Silas to be in the neighborhood. If he doesn't show up by Friday, I'm going to have to take measures into my own hands."

"Julia, don't you go cutting your grass. You'll have a stroke or something."

"I'm not going to. What I mean is, I'll have to find someone to get over here and do it for me."

"Well, since I moved, I don't have to worry about grass cutting. That's one good thing."

14

Julia's Birthday

John found out it was a muscle. The "shaman" had that pretty well diagnosed, but she was not going to say another word or she would probably burst out laughing again. Janine had to laugh at herself for being so joyful these days. It was a real change of attitude.

After John took some muscle relaxants he felt much better. The doctor said he should use ice off and on for the rest of the day and could use heat later in the evening.

The week went by without too much happening, which was fine with both of them. Janine was back to walking, and John just took it easy for a change.

Sunday morning, John seemed fine, and they were eager to get to church. Kevin Kirkland met them at the door again with bulletins in hand. "Good morning, John," he said.

"Good morning, Kevin. It's nice to see you."

"How are you after your exercise of last Sunday?"

"Good. It was a mighty fine day. We both enjoyed it tremendously."

"We did too. We haven't had a ball game like that in quite a while. The talk is we need to make it an annual event."

"That sounds like a great idea, Kevin. Well, we'd better get moving here."

They went on into the sanctuary, and the pew was filled up! It looked like one entire family was seated there. Even Raymond was moved up a pew, which also was filled because that was where Maggie and her husband sat, along with another couple.

Now what? They looked around quickly to see if there was a place with someone they already knew. Time was running out.

John said, "Let's go down there in front of the lady who came in with us that first Sunday." They didn't discuss it but quickly moved into place. The prelude hadn't started yet. Actually, Francine and the choir didn't seem to be ready. They looked over the bulletin and overheard one of the ladies behind them.

"I did a crazy thing yesterday . . . I decided to teach myself to play the piano, so I bought myself an electronic keyboard for my eighty-sixth birthday."

Janine didn't mean to listen in on someone's conversation, but the lady wasn't speaking softly and she heard what she said. *How about that? She must be a determined individual to decide on doing something so challenging at her age.* She tried to focus on the service and the message but found herself drifting off to the words the lady had said.

Even the service itself caused her to think about older people and their abilities. The pastor was talking about people of older age accomplishing great things.

Julia was thinking, *Jenny probably thinks I've lost my mind . . . Maybe I have.*

Julia wasn't paying much attention to Pastor Daniel—she still had the foolish thought on her mind about playing the piano. *I shouldn't have told anyone.* Surely, people would laugh at her if they knew.

Julia suddenly realized she needed to listen to Pastor Daniel. *The bulletin says Never Too Old. What? Never too old? Well, that's ridiculous! I'm too old for lots of things. Maybe too old to play the piano too.*

He quoted from Genesis about Sarah having a baby. She was ninety years old when Isaac was born. *Good grief!* Then he was on to talking about Noah being an old man when he built the ark.

Well, I'm not going to build an ark, and I'm not going to have a baby at the age of ninety, that's for sure. Not a chance in the world.

Pastor Daniel had said to *her*—was he looking straight at *her?* "The Bible reveals that age is never a barrier to our being used by God. Is there something that you want to do? Do you feel that God has called you to it for some reason? You have a purpose for this. Pray for God's help and do it."

She felt her face turn red, and she looked down at her arthritic hands. *All things are possible with God,* she thought. *All things? I wonder.*

Janine thought of the lady behind her as Pastor Daniel was giving his message. She made up her mind. She was going to speak to her about piano lessons. After all, she had taught for years and knew she could help her. If the lady tried to do it on her own, she would never get it right and become frustrated instead of enjoying a new undertaking.

Everyone was standing. The pastor was giving the benediction and people started moving from their seats. Julia couldn't seem to move and was still thinking of how he had been looking straight at her.

"Julia, are you all right?" Jenny asked.

"Of course," she answered, pulling herself together. Just then, the new lady who was sitting in the pew in front of her with her husband introduced herself to her.

"My name's Janine Stephens."

"Hello, I'm Julia Gillanders, and this is Jenny McMurray. You're new here."

"Yes. We are . . . I want to tell you that I overheard you talking about purchasing an electronic keyboard and teaching yourself how to play it."

Oh no! Even this person I don't even know thinks I'm a crazy old woman. The lady said she had taught piano for many years and offered to give her lessons. Free.

Julia was oversensitive and uncomfortable as a result of Pastor Daniel looking at her and preaching at her, and now here was this complete stranger making her an offer. *I don't even know her. How can I possibly trust her anyway?* "I'll have to think about it," she said, not wanting to take the time to get in a discussion with her and hurried out of the church. She was glad to get by the pastor without pausing to shake his hand.

John said, "So . . . I thought you were finished with teaching."

"I am. I am. This is different. This is just helping somebody out."

"Um-hm."

Lucy came down from the choir loft and greeted the Stephens. Francine didn't hurry past today but instead asked them if they enjoyed the day last week. She said that she and Lawrence certainly did, and even though they didn't play ball, they felt they were pretty good cheerleaders.

"Everyone had a good time," Janine said.

Maggie asked John if he had trouble getting out of bed the next morning.

"Oh, no. I got along just fine."

Janine looked over her glasses at him and didn't say a word.

They were driving home, and Janine asked him if he had told a lie about feeling well on Monday.

He said he didn't. He said that Maggie had asked him if he had trouble getting out of bed and he said he got along just fine. "I didn't have trouble getting out of bed. I just had trouble standing up."

She was satisfied.

When Julia and Jenny got in the car after church services, Julia asked, "Jenny, what do you think about that new woman?"

"I don't know. She seems nice. Why?"

"Well, she said she'd teach me to play the piano. I don't want someone to teach me. I'm sure I can teach myself. Anyway, these old arthritic fingers are going to have a hard enough time at it. I don't need someone hovering over me, trying to get me to do something I don't want to do or can't do."

"Well, that's up to you," Jenny said, "but she seems like a sincere person, and maybe you could just give it a short try and see what happens."

"Harrumph! Are we going to go to lunch today?"

"Fine with me. I have no reason to go on home."

Jenny drove them a half mile out the country road to the Orchard Restaurant, a good place for a home-cooked meal or cup of soup after church or any time. The widowed ladies gathered there often on Sundays, partly to delay going to an empty house for the rest of the week. Iola, Beatrice, and Harriet were already seated in the small separate dining area when Julia and Jenny arrived.

They were all chattering over this and that, and no one said that they noticed the preacher talking about Julia today. *Well, they know he was. But they are not going to say anything so as not to make me uncomfortable.* She ordered a cup of chicken noodle soup and tried to calm herself down.

ᎩᎩᎩ

John read the entire Sunday paper. He liked to do that, and it usually took half of the day. All of a sudden, he realized what time it was and that he hadn't heard from Janine for hours. "Hey! Janine! Where are you?"

"I'm downstairs. I'll be up pretty soon."

He got up and walked around. Goodness, his back was getting stiff.

She came up, and he said, "Would you like to take a little stroll? I think I could use it."

"Sure, I'll go get my shoes."

They were walking toward where their daughter lived. Maybe they'd stop over and say "Hi."

"What were you doing all afternoon?" he asked her.

"I was digging around, trying to locate those boxes with the piano lesson music in them. I know I kept them."

"I think you got rid of all of them."

"No . . . Are you sure?"

"You said you were never going to need them again. Remember?"

"Oh, darn. You're right. Now if Julia decides to trust me to help her, I'll have to go get new music. John, I knew I shouldn't throw anything out. That's what happens. Keep something for years, and as soon as you get rid of it, you're going to need it."

"Well, she may not want to have you do this anyway."

"I can run to town in a jiffy and get anything I need from the music store if it becomes necessary, and now I can at least stop searching for the old ones."

They walked past the little farmhouse, and the couple was out on the porch waving. They were adorable. They decided that this time, they would stop and say a few words to them. They walked toward the porch, and the old folks immediately jumped up and greeted them gladly.

"Hello there. We've walked by and seen you before and decided it was time to stop and introduce ourselves. I'm John Stephens and this is my wife, Janine."

"Wonderful! Wonderful! We are happy to meet you. I'm Abraham and this is my wife, Sarah."

"No kidding!" John just couldn't help himself. He wished he hadn't said that.

Abraham just laughed and slapped his leg. "That's what everyone does."

"Well, it must have been in the Lord's plan when your parents named you," Janine said. "It's good to meet you."

"Won't you sit a spell?"

"Sure. Thanks."

"Been walkin' far?"

"No, we live just a ways down there. We bought the Stafford property."

"Nice place. I hope you'll be happy," Sarah finally spoke. "You must be thirsty. Can I get you a drink of water?"

"No, thanks. We're going to be walking on down to our daughter's home in a bit. Have you met Kathy or Greg Lang or their daughters?"

"Meghan?"

"Yes. She's our granddaughter."

"She's a right nice youngin. She rides by here on her bicycle and comes to talk with us."

Meghan would do that. John and Janine were glad. These poor old folks probably appreciate a nice young girl visiting with them.

"How long have you folks lived here?"

Sarah looked at Abe. He said, "Maybe fifty years, give or take a few."

"Well, it seems like a good place to be. I think we'll get on to our daughter's. Maybe we can visit again sometime," John stood. So did Janine.

They smiled, and she said, "Come again."

When they got out of sight, Janine said, "Sarah and Abraham?"

They sure got a charge out of that. They forgot to ask their last names.

Prince knew they were coming before anyone else possibly could. He bounded up with greetings, and all three of them went to the house. They only stayed long enough to get a cool drink of water. Janine did tell Kathy that she saw Maggie again this morning. "She always asks about you."

"She's very special," said Kathy.

"Oh, and another thing . . . There was this lady sitting behind us this morning, talking with her friend. She said she is eighty-six years old and is going to teach herself to play the piano. What do you think about that?"

"My goodness! Isn't it just wonderful that she wants to do something like that at her age?"

"Your mother thinks she could use her help."

"No doubt about that. Are you going to help her, Mother?"

"She has to decide. I offered, but she is a little leery of me. I don't blame her. She doesn't know anything about me at all, so can she trust me not to steal her blind or be a good person? She'll probably let me know next Sunday. It might be fun."

"Hey! Have you ever talked with the old couple who has the farm?" John asked.

"I haven't, but Meghan has made friends with them. Why?"

"Do you know their names?" John asked.

"Actually, no."

"Abraham and Sarah."

"No! What are the chances of that happening?"

"Maybe they are Jewish. Then there would be a better chance of it happening."

"I guess. That's really remarkable, isn't it? What's the last name?"

"We don't know. Well, we'd better get along. Stop over any time."

They hurried on home and didn't see Abe and Sarah on the return trip. They kept discovering the most interesting things!

15

Telephone Gossip

"Hello, Julia. I just spoke to Jenny. I hope you don't mind that she told me what Mrs. Stephens said to you yesterday."

"I can't believe that the entire community now knows of the crazy thing I have done. Iola, I never dreamed that people would be this interested in me. I wish they weren't," Julia said.

"It's not just that, Julia. Oh, I think it's fine that you are going to get into playing the piano. You know what Reverend Campbell said on Sunday: 'You're never too old.'"

"Iola, I am not interested in this conversation. I am very, very uncomfortable with this right now. I know what Reverend Daniel said, and I know that he was looking straight at me, but I still have my own decision to make here. Please. Is there something else you'd like to talk about?"

"In a minute. Please listen to this one thing, first: Reverend Campbell was not speaking directly to you. Sometimes the preachers are called to speak on a certain subject, and maybe his message was a bit for you and a bit for all of us older people. I thought he was talking to me as well. But what I really wanted to ask . . . Did Mrs. Stephens actually say she was a piano teacher?"

"Oh my! I don't like talking about anybody."

"That's not talking about anybody. If she told you that, she meant for people to know it. She's not keeping it a secret."

"She said she *had* taught piano lessons for many years."

"Aha! That's great. She's a musician. We need her kind around here. Well, listen, you do what you feel you should do. That's up to you. Maybe the Lord wants you to get to know Mrs. Stephens for some reason unknown to us."

ϒϒϒ

"Hi, Francine. Did you hear?" Laura was calling.

"Hear what?"

"The new lady at church—she's a musician."

"You don't say? What kind of a musician?"

"She has taught piano for one thing."

"Well, this is certainly interesting. I wonder if she sings."

"Of course!"

"How do you know?"

"Well, that's what I heard."

"Maybe she'll join the choir. We can always use more people in the choir."

"Maybe she would direct the choir for you."

"Now there's a good thought."

"Well, better go. See you soon. Bye."

ᐱᐱᐱ

"Hello, Adele. Did you hear?" Beatrice asked.

"Hear what?"

"That new lady, Mrs. Stephens, she's going to open up a piano studio in West Hope."

"Well, I didn't even know she played piano."

"Well, she does, and she's going to start teaching."

"How do you know?"

"Jenny told me she talked with Julia about teaching." Bea was delighted to be passing along such interesting information.

"Where will she have her studio?"

"I was wondering the same thing. There's that empty building that used to be the bicycle shop. It probably could be fixed up just right for a music studio."

"Maybe . . . We sure could see more culture around here."

"Well, time will tell, I guess."

ᐱᐱᐱ

On Thursday morning, the secretary of Hope Church received a telephone call from one of the members.

"Hello, Georgia. How are things?"

"Good. Who's this?"

"Oh, sorry. It's Rebecca Armtridge."

"Hi, Becky. I didn't recognize your voice."

"That's okay. I need to get in touch with the new lady in church, Mrs. Stephens. Do you have a phone number for her?"

"I do, but I'm not allowed to give it out. It was given to us in confidence."

"Oh, darn. I wanted to call her about teaching piano lessons to Shirley."

"Piano lessons?"

"Yes, she's going to open up a studio here in West Hope, and I want to be early on the list."

"Well, that's wonderful. I'm sorry I can't help you. Perhaps you will see her in church on Sunday."

"I guess that means I'd better attend this week, right?"

"Good thinking. See you then."

During Sunday school, Julia confessed about her keyboard. She might as well; everyone seemed to know about it anyway.

"Mrs. Stephens said she'd come to teach me piano lessons if I want her to. She used to teach," she said.

"Used to?" asked Bea.

"Yes, that's what she said."

"She didn't say you could come to her new studio?" Anne asked.

"Nothing about a studio."

"Hmm. Well, I heard she is opening up a studio," said Iola.

"So, what are you going to do, Julia?"

"I think I've decided to go with it for a while. I'm not crazy about having someone push me into practices and watching my fingers on the keys and so forth, but she was probably right when she said it would be very difficult for me to teach myself. I do want to learn. That probably sounds silly to you that I do, but I decided that I'd better do it now and not put it off any longer."

"I'm like that too. I say if you want to do something . . . then do it," Bea interjected.

Well, everyone knew Bea was like that, but this was out of character for Julia, who had been so quiet and just went along with everybody all the time.

"By the way, Bea, did you find any aches and pains on Monday?" Laura asked.

"Oh, boy did I! But you know what I told myself?"

"What?"

"I said, 'Bea Roberts, every time you have one of those pains, just remember how much fun you had gettin' it.' I had lots of reminders."

They all laughed at that.

When they went to the sanctuary, Julia and Jenny went over to their normal place. Julia was looking for the Stephenses. She was thinking they weren't coming today, but in they came and sat down in front of them.

A lot of people were looking toward Janine. Rumors had pretty much gotten all around the borough and outlying areas about the music studio (which Janine herself knew nothing about). Janine turned around and greeted the two ladies who looked especially beautiful this morning.

Jenny had on her pink suit. Janine was happy to see her in it while being able to identify the person. Julia had a very pretty floral skirt, beige blouse, and a jacket of blue that matched one of the colors in the skirt. She wore fashionable custom jewelry and a big lapel pin. Both ladies used makeup and had very pretty white hair.

The music started, so Janine would wait until after services to talk again with Julia.

Why were the choir members looking at her that way? Janine couldn't figure it out. When they would catch her eye, they would smile, knowingly . . . *Knowingly?*

Yes, they must know something I don't know. Maybe they are thinking I'm a lucky woman to have such a handsome husband with a great personality and sportsmanship. She smiled within and decided not to catch anyone's eye anymore.

After the benediction, she turned, and Julia quickly said, "I decided to go ahead with the lessons with you. Thank you. When would we begin?"

Janine was shocked. She had rehearsed a statement she would give when Julia said she had decided to do it herself.

"Wonderful! Where do you live?"

"Just down the hill and on the main street here. It's easy to find." She went on to tell her the address.

"How about Tuesday morning at ten o'clock? Would that work for you?"

Julia was thinking that she had every morning and every afternoon free, but she responded, "That would be fine."

"I'll find us some books and bring them along and see you on Tuesday."

Others were waiting their turn to talk with Janine. Next was Francine.

"Janine, if you'd like to come sing in the choir, we would love to have you."

Janine had decided firmly that she would not do that. She didn't know for sure what the Lord wanted her to do here at Hope Church, and she would not decide for Him.

"Thank you very much. I think I'd better take my time for a while."

Francine was disappointed but didn't say any more.

Bea was next. "Good morning!"

"Well, here's our softball star. Good morning! You gave us a good time last week. I hope you know that."

"I hear you're opening up a music studio. Is that right?" The ladies had put her up to it.

"What? No, that is not right. I used to teach music, but I am retired from that now. There are other things I must do." She didn't know what, but it was the right answer.

"Oh. Well, sometimes in a small community like this, things get going like the old 'gossip' game. Sorry to upset you."

"No. You didn't upset me, but you sure caught me off guard with that."

Then a young woman and two children were waiting. She introduced herself as Rebecca Armtridge, and her two children were Shirley and Doug.

"I just wanted to get my daughter, Shirley, on the list for piano lessons at your new studio."

Good grief! I can't believe this! She looked over at John who was holding back a laugh. *He shouldn't be laughing when I'm in such a jam here.*

"Well, believe me, if I were going to have a studio and if I were going to be teaching again, I would be happy to have Shirley as a student. I have retired from teaching. I'm sorry. I hope there will be someone else to teach your little girl."

Shirley looked pretty disappointed, but Janine was not going to let that influence her! No way!

If all this had not happened, she would have been a happy woman that day. She was happy about Julia, but the studio thing was crazy . . . *or was it?* She brushed that thought from her mind immediately and began fixing dinner for John and herself. They enjoyed eating their heavier meal early on Sunday, freeing up the day for adventures or relaxation. They would later decide to take a drive along a road to the south to get a better perspective of the community.

As they turned onto the road, they were immediately transported to farmlands with wheat waving their heads, cattle quietly chewing their cud, fields of corn nearly ready to be picked, and an occasional dog barking at the interruption of an automobile upon his tranquil existence.

As they rounded a bend on the narrow, two-lane road, they came upon a field of sheep. A few were close to the road. "I had no idea that a sheep was that large," Janine remarked.

"Those pictures of sheep and shepherds from the children's Bible stories are about as close as I have come to seeing one, except at a zoo. There's that petting zoo over in West Virginia we want to take the boys next time they come. They also have goats there. I don't want to get near a goat! I hear they will 'buck' into you."

A man was walking in the field with the sheep, actually holding a crook! What a sight! They were suddenly transported back in time as well as to the scenic countryside.

"Janine, would you have believed that we were living this close to a completely different way of life? This is amazing!"

"Nice."

"There's a sign on the mailbox there. See if it is a name we know."

Janine read, "Davidson."

"I don't think I've met anyone by that name, but I do recall reading, either in the church bulletin or the newsletter, the Scottish name. I think it was in the bulletin that Sunday. What a nice farm! Looks like they have Black Angus cattle."

They hadn't been traveling more than twenty minutes on the country road when they came to an intersection of a dirt road, and John decided to go exploring.

They both sensed that they might be on private property although there wasn't a sign to indicate that. They were going to turn around when they came upon a small village. Welcome to Bryston, the old, weathered sign read. The houses were closely lined together on both sides of the main road, as well as projecting outward on side streets in the same fashion. John said it looked like an old mining community. The houses were as weathered as the sign, and there was little sign of life within them. A few dogs ran out to the auto, and they were baring their teeth in anger at the strangers. Janine quickly put her window up when a very large dog lunged at her, and she emphatically declared that they had better get away from there *right now!*

As they turned around and headed back the way they had come, John saw in the rearview mirror that there were people back at the settlement, and from what he could see of them, they were not the kind you would want to meet. Four men were standing smack in the middle of the road, facing the car with movements of others behind.

"Good heavens!" Janine said. "What on earth did we run into?"

"Whew! I'm sure I don't know, but I'll tell you this—we won't be back! From now on, we stay on the main roads."

"I'll tell you, John, this city gal got a real scare out of that!"

"They could have been moonshining. I've heard stories about people like that. They shoot at those who do not have what they determine is a legitimate reason to be in their territory."

"Legitimate? I suppose you mean 'buying.' I can't believe it! It's our own fault. We're old enough to know better, but honestly, I never gave a thought to something like this."

They passed the Davidson's and the grazing sheep and were coming back to West Hope and turned toward Innesport to get ice-cream cones. The country store in West Hope would not be open on a Sunday. They were soon on their way back toward McCade Road, a little more comfortable but anxious from the strange encounter.

"We are strangers in a new land, John. Up until now, it's been nothing but good, but we know that life is not all like that. We'll want to be sure that we are on the right path from now on." Having said that, she applied it to her journey to West Hope and realized that she would have to "follow the Leader" very carefully so as not to wander away from the rightful path there as well.

When they reached their home, Janine told John that she wanted to think about how to begin the piano lessons for Julia. Tomorrow she would go to the music store in Innesport. She knew it had been years since she'd had the pleasure of teaching an adult. She had found over the years that when an adult set out to learn something, the student would give the project much more time and attention than would a child. Was that because that person didn't want to embarrass herself or because she felt that time was short and she needed to make the most of it? Nevertheless, she felt it would be a pleasure to teach this nice old lady, and she looked forward to getting started on Tuesday.

16

Familiarities

Julia was awake most of the night, nervous and apprehensive about whether or not she could learn anything at this stage of her life. *I know everything about me has slowed down, so I suppose it will be a problem for me to understand quickly enough, and I'm sure I will have trouble getting these old fingers to move on the piano keys.*

Mrs. Stephens is gonna be sorry she ever talked with me. I wish I had just said "no" to this whole idea. Who cares if I learn the piano? Who will I play for anyway? No one, and that's for sure. I wanted to play for me! Who was I kidding? I'm fooling myself, that's who.

She decided to get up for the day at 6:00 a.m.—earlier than usual. She never slept much past six anymore. It would take her a long time to get dressed and be ready for Mrs. Stephens at ten o'clock. She struggled out of bed, sat on the side until she felt her bearings, slipped into her slippers, and flip-flopped across to the bathroom.

After bathing, brushing teeth and hair, and putting on some makeup, she went back to the bedroom and sat in a chair to rest awhile. When she felt like she could handle it, she took her panty hose back from the chair and began the painstaking process of getting her feet and legs into them. It was easier when she had those knee hose, but they wouldn't stay up anymore on her skinny legs.

She rolled the left panty leg all the way to the toes and, while seated, bent over, and just barely reaching her toes, wiggled them into the hose. She pulled that side up to the ankle and proceeded to roll the right foot to the toe. Now she had to have both feet on the floor while reaching over to work the right foot into the stocking. By the time she had both feet fully covered to her ankles, she was worn out! She sat back in the chair with the stockings still at her ankles, took several deep breaths, and shook her shoulders and neck to loosen them up.

Finally, she felt as though she could continue, so bending over and taking hold of both sides of the panty hose, she pulled one side and then the other until both were to her knees. Standing was a bit of a problem because the stockings were very tight around her knees. She felt as though she were lassoed around the legs and would flop over, but she kept her balance. She managed to work the panty hose all the way to her waist. Again, she sat down. This time she dropped both arms and shook them around, breathed deeply, and stayed that way for a few minutes.

Now to the slacks! She put them on the floor where she could put both feet into the legs of the slacks and began pulling them up both sides. This also took time, but she eventually stood with them on. She walked to where her shoes were and was berating herself for having purchased shoes with ties! She could not bear to bend over again right now. She took the shoes to the chair, loosened the strings, put both on the floor, and slid her feet into them. One at a time, she grunted her body over long enough to tie each shoe.

She looked at the clock. It was past seven already. She needed a drink of water and drank from the bottle beside her bed. As always, she pulled the covers in place and straightened the bed. She went to the closet and took out the blouse she had planned to wear this day, put it on, and buttoned it. When she looked in the mirror, she saw a tired old lady.

My goodness! This getting old is harder than most people realize. I feel like I've already put in a whole day's work. She inched her way downstairs, holding on to the banister all the way.

By the time she fixed her breakfast, ate, and cleaned up her bowl, plate, and spoon, it was nine o'clock. Mrs. Stephens would be here in an hour! *I need to put on some lipstick, go unlock the front door, pick up the newspaper from yesterday, and anything else that needs a little straightening up.*

She finally plopped down on her chair at nine thirty and hoped she wasn't too tired to stay awake while Mrs. Stephens was there. She nodded off to sleep and awoke with a start. *What time is it?* It was nine forty-five, which was still fine.

I'd better get up and get my circulation going. She paced the floor between the living room and dining room. It was a good thing that Janine came five minutes early, or she would have been tired from pacing.

$\curlyvee\curlyvee\curlyvee$

She opened the door and invited Janine inside. Amenities were exchanged, and Julia invited Janine to the back of the house where the keyboard was located.

Surprisingly, it was a fine keyboard. The salesman had not taken advantage of her. Julia had it sitting on a table of about the correct height for her to reach the keys. A small stool sat in front of it.

Janine wanted to get a feel for the keys and said "May I?" as she indicated the keyboard.

"Oh, sure. Go ahead." She was glad she didn't have to start just yet.

Janine played over it without being too elaborate with anything and said, "Mrs. Gillanders, this is a fine keyboard. I think it will work very well for you."

Julia was relieved because she was not so sure about it. "I'd like for you to call me Julia."

Janine was glad for that and told her to call her Janine.

They talked for a while about the settings. Janine wanted her to see where the "piano" setting was because there were settings for organ, harpsichord, celesta, and other instruments as well. If Julia pushed one of the buttons by mistake, she might become frustrated. With that settled, they talked about finger positioning.

The shape of Julia's poor old fingers saddened Janine. She didn't care as far as her playing was concerned but felt sorry for any pain she might have or feel during playing. She knew

Julia was embarrassed but acted as though she hadn't noticed the crookedness of the fingers. She proceeded to work with her about using the proper finger on each individual key.

Janine didn't give her too much to do for the week and suggested that she should try to practice for at least twenty minutes each day. There were sheets of questions she could answer concerning basic understanding of musical notation, note values, etc. "If you would have time to answer those, it would be great."

Julia asked her if she would like to sit awhile, and Janine was very happy for that. Janine told her she recently moved to McCade Road from Innesport and that her husband had retired from a corporation that had downsized. She said that their daughter lived on Bear Track Lane, and they were happy to be near her. She didn't lie, and she didn't go into any detail whatsoever about the real reason they moved into the Stafford home. There would be a more appropriate time to do that, she hoped.

Janine did most of the talking, hoping to ease Julia's mind. An unknown woman was now entering her home regularly. Janine knew she herself would not be comfortable with a complete stranger as a "home teacher" either.

They both got a giggle out of the gossip that spread throughout the community concerning Janine opening up a music studio. Julia assured her that she did not start that rumor, and Janine told her she was certain of that. It was the old telephone story that gathered up a new word with each messenger.

"Julia, I think I should get on home. It's been a pleasure being with you today. I hope you will enjoy playing the piano. I wouldn't know what to do without playing mine. Practice when you can and I'll be back next Tuesday. I'll see you on Sunday though."

"Oh, yes, I guess you will. I hope you like Hope Church. We all think it's just fine and are pleased that you are coming there too. Thank you."

"You're welcome, Julia. Bye."

Janine left thinking, *What a lovely lady. I think we'll get along very well together.*

Julia thought, *She's very nice. She didn't seem upset with my fumblings and was very patient. This might work . . . It actually might.*

She was relieved, and her anxieties were completely lifted; however, now she was ready for a nap! She turned on the television for company, leaned back in her recliner, and was asleep in no time. She dreamed pleasant dreams about Maypoles, dancing, and beautiful music.

She was awakened an hour later by the ringing of the telephone. When she finally realized it was ringing, she picked it up from the side table by the recliner.

"Hello!"

"Hello! How was the lesson?"

It was Iola, of course. She would have to know.

"Fine."

"Fine? That really doesn't say much."

"Well, it was! Janine is very nice."

"Oh, it's Janine, is it?"

"Yes. They moved here from Innesport. Her husband is retired, and their daughter lives on Bear Track Lane. She seems happy to be out of the city."

"So you think she'll stay at Hope Church?"

"Yes, I do. She seems to like it there."

"With her musical talents, she can be a great help to us."

"Yes, Iola, but we shouldn't rush her into anything. We might scare her away. I'm sure she will want to do something in the church in time."

"Oh, I know. I'm not going to try to get her to do anything."

"Iola, please remember you said that. You always try to get people to do things in the church. I know you want to help the church, but this time, it would be better to wait. I can sense that it would be best. I don't know why, but I'm sure that if you say anything too soon, it would be the wrong thing to do."

Iola was absolutely stunned. When did Julia become outspoken? She hasn't expressed such a strong opinion in all the years she'd known her.

"Julia, I think you're right. Let's wait and see and pray for the best."

ᴎᴎᴎ

Janine decided to stop at the country store, mostly to see what was inside. Elda was busying herself with wiping down shelves. Hayden, behind the counter, greeted her.

"Hello, ma'am. Can I get something for you?"

"Hello. I think I know what I need. I'll look over here a moment." She hadn't the slightest idea what she would pick up to cover the fact that she didn't need a thing.

She walked through all the aisles, amazed that the little store had a pretty fine stock of items. Kathy was right. Almost anything she would need would be here.

She decided that a jar of homemade apple butter would be yummy, and she'd get a box of crackers to go with that. She also picked up a homemade candle that had the fragrance of a lily and a brand-new Pilot pen—her favorite!

Hayden had gone to the back, and Elda moved over to check her out.

"Do you like lilies?" asked Elda.

"Yes, I really do. I think my favorite floral scent is a peony though."

"Oh, yes! We have some next door. I agree. You can hardly find better than the beautiful fragrance of a peony."

"Are you from around here?"

"Yes, as a matter of fact. We only recently moved out on McCade Road."

"You are Mrs. Stephens?"

Janine was shocked to hear her speak her name! She wasn't familiar with the small-town way of life where "everybody knows everybody else."

"Yes, I am Mrs. Stephens . . . Forgive me, I don't think I know your name."

Elda extended her hand to Janine and told Janine her name and her husband's.

"It's nice to meet you. I'll tell you one thing I know. You are a wonderful baker. My daughter served me some of your fresh-baked bread one day. It was delicious."

"Thank you. It's one of the pleasures of life—baking . . . So I suppose you've been over to Ms. Julia's?"

Again, Janine was surprised. *This is going to take some getting used to.* "Yes, we had a good morning together. She's a lovely lady."

"She certainly is. Taking piano lessons, is she?"

Janine was becoming uncomfortable with this conversation; she felt things were getting much too personal. In all her life, she had not belonged to a community or church organization where everyone knew everyone's business. In her former community, people came together from various parts of the city, and their personal lives were their own. She felt that she shouldn't say anything more about Ms. Julia to a third party.

"I guess everyone knows about that . . . You know, I really must be getting on my way. My husband will be thinking I'm lost. It was nice to meet you both. I'm sure I'll be seeing you again soon."

At that, she was out the door and was relieved to be finished with the conversation. The proprietors were very nice. It wasn't that.

She got into the car, started the engine, drove a mile or so, and pulled off the road to consider this newest of situations. *Now then . . . It is a very small community. They probably know one another so well that they feel like family to one another. That's a good thing . . . Families are good.*

Some family members might be much too nosy and ask a lot of questions . . . and interfere with our lives . . . and circulate private information that would cause embarrassment.

On the other hand, families will protect one another . . . and be helpful to each other in times of need . . . Jesus has taught us to protect and be helpful. "Love one another as I have loved you." He didn't say that we should keep our distance.

OK . . . The love wins out. I'm going to have to work very hard at this, but I will make a sincere effort to adjust to this culture of closeness.

She came home to an empty house. John had left her a note, saying he had gone to buy gasoline for the lawnmower and that he wouldn't be long. She was disappointed. He was her buddy—her best friend—and she wanted to tell him all about Julia, the lesson, and the meeting with Elda and Hayden in the store. Oh well, she'd see him soon.

17

S Is for Stephens

Janine picked up last Sunday's bulletin, which she had saved. There on the standard insert was Edward Davidson's name as a Sunday school teacher. *I knew I saw that name somewhere.* She had begun making notes on her bulletin concerning the people she had met or names she had heard to help her differentiate one from another.

She began thinking about their near mishap last Sunday on their investigative drive. *That was positively frightening. I suppose every community has clusters of people who might not be desirable or trustworthy contacts. I know Innesport definitely has them.* She had become familiar with those places in her life and avoided going into such neighborhoods, but the rural life seemed so peaceful and safe. Coming upon a wayside community without expecting to do so, being attacked by vicious dogs, and seeing sinister-looking men in the rearview mirror was truly haunting. *Someday, I'll ask someone about that situation.*

On a Sunday in September, Julia and her friend Jenny promptly spoke to the Stephenses. As always, they said "Good morning" and nothing more. It was a hot morning for September with no air stirring. The ceiling fans were turned on but didn't seem to change a thing in the temperature of the sanctuary. There were beautifully decorated fans in every pew, something Janine remembered from her youth but hadn't seen for a long time. Victorian-style pictures of beautiful flowers in deep colors were on some of the fans, while others had the loving portrait of "The Good Shepherd" depicted upon them. She used hers and thought it was charmingly pleasant.

On Sundays past, one complete pew in the center had been filled from end to end, but this morning, only half of that pew was being used. Even so, the church seemed fuller the past two Sundays since the children had returned to school and vacations were ending. Faces were becoming familiar, but the Stephenses still only knew a few members by name. Regardless of that, they were feeling quite comfortable as regulars even though they had not as yet decided to transfer their membership.

During the announcements, someone stood and urged everyone to be sure to mark their calendars for the second Saturday in October for October Fest and that there was more information in this month's newsletter available for pickup. The announcement certainly piqued Janine and John's curiosity, and they would be picking up one of the newsletters for the "guests" this morning.

They went over to the alphabetically arranged newsletters and looked to the back of the box where "guests" were placed and were interrupted by Raymond who said there was one with their names on it in the *S* stack. *Well, how nice! A very pleasant surprise.*

18

The Teacher

Julia would say she learned so much from Janine as Janine came to her house every week to teach piano. Julia was eager to learn and practiced very seriously. They would spend at least thirty minutes at lessons and then, for another hour or more, they would go to the living room and talk about the neighborhood and the church. In view of the fact that Janine did not live in West Hope, she learned from Julia about the people, family connections, and histories as Julia became *her* teacher.

"Julia, have you always lived in West Hope?" Janine asked one day.

"Oh no," she said. "I came here after I married Andrew. His family always lived here. They were a bit high class, the Gillanders. I don't think they ever really accepted me as part of the family. I was not up to their standards, I suppose. I came from the other side of the tracks in a coal-mining community but attended the same school as Andrew." She had a smile and seemed to travel back in time as she spoke. "I can't believe to this day that Andrew ever looked my way. He was the star football player, and his family had property. But for some reason, he did.

"We moved in with his family at first and then got a place of our own. I always tried to do everything I could to help out with the family. I took care of those who were sick even when I was teaching school and taking care of my own children because I wanted them to like me and be happy that Andrew had married me. I probably never did convince them all, but anyway, I tried."

"You taught school?"

"Yes, I did. Would you believe that my father sent me to college? Here I was, a child of immigrants . . . Actually, I was the fourth child. The others were not sent to college, but my father insisted that I go . . . Anyway, someone had talked to him about me and said that they could arrange for me to go to Wills College and I could work there and help pay for my tuition and so forth. I was scared to death, but if my father thought I should do it, I would.

"I worked my way through school. We only had to have two years of college in those days to be a teacher. Looking back, I guess it wasn't such a terribly long time, even though it seemed to me to be."

"Did you start teaching right away? You must have been barely twenty years old."

"Well, I did. It was terrible! I was more frightened than the children, but I was determined that they would not know it. Somehow, and I don't know how, I made it through that first year and stayed with teaching until retirement."

"I heard you say you had children."

"We had three. The first one didn't make it after a few days. A couple of years later, we had another boy. And later we had a daughter."

"Oh, Julia, I'm sorry you lost a child. That's one of the worst experiences there can be."

"Well, what can you do? Sometimes life is hard. *Most* of the time, life is hard, really. But we have to face up to the problems we have and not let them pull us down so far, we can't get up again. I was very thankful that Charlie lived, and later, God gave us Ruthie, so we were blessed for sure. Sometimes I felt like I wasn't a very good mother."

"Oh, I can't believe that."

"Well, I really don't think so . . . I tried . . . I really did. But it seemed I gave more attention to my students than to my own children. It was a busy time, coming home and fixing supper, grading papers, and so forth. I hope I gave my children all that I should have or could have. I often sit and think about it, and I hope and pray I didn't let them down."

"Julia, we all do our best. It's all we can do. Don't look back and worry about something like that. Are your children happy? Where are they?"

"Charlie is in Portland, Maine. He has two children. Their pictures are over there. And Ruthie is in Indiana, teaching school. They are both fine and doing well, I guess. I don't see much of them, but they do call and visit when they can." She seemed to drift off into another time and place. It was apparent that she missed her children.

"Well, it's great that you live in such a wonderful, close-knit community and have many friends."

"Yes, that is the truth. We've known one another around here for a long, long time and have shared a lot. Janine, this is a good place to live. It's quiet and peaceful here until those noisy trucks go zooming by. And the people around here really care about one another. You know, if I get up in the middle of the night and turn on a light in the bedroom or what have you, someone the next day is going to ask me if I'm all right. Emily across the street and her husband never miss a chance to check up on me. I'm a widow and alone, but not . . . if you know what I mean."

"That must certainly be comforting, Julia. I'm learning more about your community and neighbors every day, and it's such a good thing for me. Thanks for sharing. Well, I'd better get on home. Time just flies by when we get to talk, and I wish it didn't have to stop. I'll see you in church and also next Tuesday, God willing."

Julia sat there for a long time after Janine went home. It was good to have a new friend. *Things haven't changed much around here for a long time, unless someone dies or something like that. And there sure isn't much to get excited about. But hey! I'm learning to play the piano. That's something new. I'll get some more practicing in after a while. Maybe a little nap would be good.*

19

An Apple for the Teacher

On Tuesday, Julia greeted Janine rather enthusiastically, which was rather out of character for Julia. She usually was quite reserved and somewhat at a distance. Janine didn't know if that was her true nature or if she had been holding back, considering their relationship as student-to-teacher. However, her attitude of friendliness warmed Janine's heart. Julia had a very good lesson. She obviously practiced every day; her fingers seemed to be loosening and moving over the keys without struggle.

Julia smiled when she finished playing for Janine, showing pride in herself.

"Congratulations, Julia! That was very good. You are practicing a lot, I can tell."

"Yes, I am. I enjoy it. Sometimes when I get bored, I just come in here and go over my lesson several times. I guess maybe I was *really* bored this week." She laughed. Janine had never seen her laugh before. As she did, her face lit up, and her eyes sparkled, emitting a joy from within. Janine thought she was truly beautiful and was so happy that she was enjoying herself. She sensed that Julia had felt very little pleasure for a long, long time. If she, Janine, could bring a little joy to another, it would make her world even better.

They moved along with the lesson and went into the living room to chat. Janine mentioned something about the center pew having less people now, and Julia said, "Oh, yes! Those are the Severights. Some of their grandchildren were here for the summer months to help out at the apple orchard. They had to go back to school and home. Nice family. Marcia and Marvin have that orchard. They took it over from Marvin's father a long time ago. They raised their children there and taught them good lessons about hard work and responsibility. They have all turned out to be fine parents themselves. You don't see a lot of parents giving their children responsibility anymore, and I'll tell you, that's half of the trouble with the world these days."

She's certainly right about that, Janine thought.

"Well, there are more people in church these days anyway. For such a small church out in the country, so to speak, it seems to me that there are a good many members there . . . maybe one hundred, do you think?"

"Last I heard, there's about 150 members, give or take. Attendance will pick up now until Christmas Eve and then it will seem that a bomb has gone off. It will be pretty slim pickin's throughout January and February. Of course, a lot of us are getting old, and we don't like to go out in the cold or snow."

"It does appear that a large portion of the congregation is of the senior class," Janine surmised.

"That's so. Not many young people are moving in."

"You mentioned the Severights. I've never stopped in at the Orchard Restaurant. Do they sell apples?"

"They sell their apples down the lane at a big barn. You turn in right alongside of the restaurant and go down a ways. You can't miss it. Do you want to buy some?"

"I do. What kind do they have?"

"Oh, I don't know if I can say. Let's see, I know they have Empire, Rome Beauty, Granny Smith, and for sure, Macintosh . . . Maybe others."

"Would you like to go with me? Maybe next Tuesday after lesson."

"I would love to. 'An apple a day, keeps the doctor away,' they say, and I sure could use all the help in that regard."

"Wonderful. We'll plan to do that . . . I have enjoyed our morning, Julia. I'll get along home and will certainly look forward to a little venture next week."

That sounded so good to Julia—a little time out of the house. "That will be very nice," she said.

ᘜᘜᘜ

"John, Julia and I are going to go to the apple orchard after lessons next Tuesday. Would you like to come with us?"

He just stood and looked at her a while. He saw the gleam in her eyes, the smile on her face, and he was touched. *I never would have thought that Janine would be so excited at such a simple proposal.* "Honey, you two go ahead. I think you would enjoy yourselves more without me tagging along. 'Too many cooks spoil the soup.'"

She smiled at that and thought, *I sure wouldn't want to spoil this soup!*

ᴦᴦᴦ

The air felt a little cooler that next Tuesday, and one could sense the coming of autumn. *This is a season for gathering apples!* Janine thought.

Janine was excited to go to the orchard with Julia. They put on their sweaters after the morning lesson, picked up their purses, and were out the door. Janine had never been to an orchard before and anticipated the fragrance of apples all around her. She was right. When they entered the barn, that's exactly what she encountered. It was intoxicatingly wonderful.

Julia was watching her, feeling a renewed joy from within as she realized the pleasure that Janine was experiencing from her first-time visit to an apple barn. Janine was surrounded with sweet fragrances, blending into God's finest. *No wonder Eve was tempted.* Janine surely had not smelled or seen anything so beautiful.

They appeared to be alone in a huge space filled with wooden boxes, approximately five-feet square and perhaps three-feet deep. They were nearly full to the top with apples of several varieties. Each box had the name of the apple and their best usage. They both walked from box to box, lifting an apple, smelling, and enjoying it.

A woman walked in and greeted them. "Hello, Julia. It's nice to see you. And this is Mrs. Stephens. Right?" *Again—that familiarity. Okay. It's going to keep happening. Just accept it.*

"Hello. Yes, I'm Janine Stephens."

"I know because I have seen you in church for some weeks now. We're glad to have you with us. I'm Marcia Severight."

"Yes, of course. I've seen you in the choir. I remember now."

"What can we do for you today?"

"I am visiting a fresh apple barn for the very first time, and what a delicious experience! I would like to get something that I could bake, and some that we can eat. What would you recommend?"

"I lot of people like the Granny Smith because they are tart and hold their form. I usually mix my apples in a pie. Are you thinking of baking pies?"

"Yes."

"Here's what I recommend: Mix equal amounts of Granny Smith, Macintosh, and either Empire, Jonagold, or Cortland. The Macintosh will cook into sauce and fill in the cracks between the slices, the Granny will stay firm, and the others will bake to a softness. All together, you will have an award-winning presentation and taste."

"And she knows. No one bakes an apple pie like Marcia," said Julia.

"Thank you, Julia. I've had many opportunities to work on those pies."

"I love to bake apple pies, but I never know what will be the end result. I never knew which apples to put into the pie," said Janine.

"Well, you might try my suggestion and let me know how they come out. As for eating, the Gala is a favorite of many, and so is the Yellow Delicious. Here, let me slice up some samples for you." She proceeded to slice along as Janine and Julia tasted. Mmm, mmm! One was as good as the rest, but Janine decided upon mixing a five-pound bag with Gala and Yellow Delicious. As for the baking, she bought five pounds each of Granny Smith, Cortland, and Macintosh. She would bake a pie today—maybe two or three. Could she ever top the "Chef"? Well, she was going to try.

On the wall behind Marcia was a life-sized print of a very proud-looking Scotsman in his red-and-black plaid kilt and complete ceremonial dress. Janine commented on it as being very impressive.

"It was a gift to Marvin, my husband. A friend gave it to him. It is depicting a gentleman of the MacKintosh clan. The Severights are part of that clan. He's become one of the family." She laughed.

"And do you all prefer the Macintosh apple?"

"Of course!"

They were all smiling, looking at the charming Scotsman gracing the room with his presence.

Janine and Julia left with bags of apples. Julia had also purchased some to eat. She didn't think she would be baking pies anymore.

"Marcia, thank you for the tastes and the tips. I'll let you know how I get along with the pies. See you in church!" Janine said.

"Thank you for coming. Come again."

"I will."

20

Janine's Prayer of Thanksgiving

"Now then, John, if yer satisfied wi'tha luunch j'est eat'n', 'ow 'boout leavin' tha premises whilst I tend to soom pie bakin'?"

"Ahhh . . . What?"

"Soom pie bakin' from the MacKintosh clan apple and a wee more of 'em."

"Girl, I can't even understand you these days. But if this means you are going to bake an apple pie if I get out of your way, then off I go!"

She kissed him on the cheek and then patted him on the behind as he went out the door.

She began humming "Annie Laurie" as she set up for the baking. This would take most of the afternoon. *So what? I don't have a meeting this evening. Ha ha! I can enjoy the baking without worrying to have to rush out somewhere. Where's that CD of bagpipe music? I'll put that on and peel and slice and roll out the dough and just have a good old time.*

She couldn't remember when she had been so at peace with her life. *Thank you, Father, for all good things.* She stopped what she was doing, sat down, and bowed her head to pray, similar to her prayers of every day.

Holy Father, Blessed Jesus, Holy Spirit, thank you for bringing me to a life I could not possibly have asked for since I didn't even know this world existed. If I had prayed for a change of direction and freshness in my life and had to specify what it would be, I would have missed this objective by miles. But through the method, Your perfect wisdom, You have brought me to a place, which has given me joy and peace.

Lord, I acknowledge that the reason for my existence is beyond my own happiness . . . I'm sure of that. Life is not to be lived for personal satisfaction, so I am expecting and waiting for You to reveal Your Plan to me. In the meantime, thank You for treating me so kindly.

Lord, I'm beginning to question with every move I make that this or that may be why I'm here, but since I am not convinced, I assume I haven't come to it yet . . . I don't want to be impatient because I know that Your time is perfect. We all have a purpose in Your Kingdom, Lord. Thank You for helping me to understand. When the time is right—in the fullness of time—I'll be here.

I love Your Word, Lord. I love the words 'in the fullness of time,' which today carry more meaning for me than ever before.

All along, I've followed my own way, thinking I was doing what was right . . . I wasn't. I know that now. Not that

I deliberately tried to do wrong. I didn't turn away from You, but I surely did not turn to You. I did not stop to listen to You calling me. I pray that You will forgive me for being so late in recognizing that this is Your world. It is not my world—I acknowledge that. Help me to serve well, fulfilling Your purpose in Your Kingdom.

Holy Spirit, when you called me to move here, I was totally convinced. I am still convinced that You will take me to that which You have for me to do.

Is Julia involved in the work You've called me to do? That's a precious thought, but I'm not pushing. Is it at Hope Church? I believe it is the focal point of my calling. Is it music? Maybe not . . . I won't step into that until I know.

Holy Lord, Three in One, in all things, thank You. I thank You for a husband who is supportive and loves You as much as I do. Again, how wonderful for me. Thank You for my family who realizes that I am telling the truth and is hopeful for me. Thank You for newness in location and friends. Thank You for revival of spirit within me.

I pray, Lord, for those I have left behind. May they follow Your path wherever You lead them. Be with them; grant that their minds and hearts will be open to hear You when You call so that they may be overflowing with hope, as I am, Lord.

Christ, be with me and lead this prayer to the Father. Amen.

21

The Best Apple Pie?

John had been raking the early leaves that floated to the ground a little at a time. The maple trees were turning quicker than the others, and there were more of them. There will be thousands and thousands of leaves to move before autumn is finished.

John had a leaf blower, but it would need a very long extension cord to reach throughout the property. He bought a big rake and set out to be faster than the falling leaves. They seemed to giggle down when he turned his back. He no sooner got every one of them swept to the woods and began to climb back up to the house when some more had fallen. It was a race! Janine silently knew who would win, and it wouldn't be John. He didn't seem to care because he loved being outside, no matter what he was doing. The move had been very good for him, and he had not once looked for another job. *Would he handle the winter months as well?* Janine wondered. Time would tell.

He entered through the kitchen door, and the aroma of baking apple pies moved him to hunger. "Mmm, mmm! Just what a hardworking man needs. A big piece of warm apple pie and some vanilla ice cream."

"Oh, really? They aren't even out of the oven yet—we'll have to wait awhile. Maybe after supper."

"No, no. Let's not wait . . . Can't we skip supper and go straight for the pie?"

"We could, but then, we'd be hungry again later."

"We could eat more pie!" He smiled. He walked over to the oven. "Can I take a peek?"

"Sure. Go ahead."

He looked inside, and there sat three perfectly beautiful pies with the letter *A* knifed into the top. Janine always did that. He couldn't remember ever smelling an apple pie that had a better aroma than these. They were almost ready! He'd go wash up.

"John, just a minute. You know you can't eat a piece of pie now. They need to cool a little and set up. Here, have a nice cool drink of water, go take a shower and a short little nap. In the meantime, I'll fix up a light supper for us, and we can crown it all off with a big piece of pie and ice cream. Maybe I'll call over to Kathy's and invite the family to join us for dessert."

"Whew! You must be very sure of your baking today to invite the Chef over."

"Yes! I am. What do you say?"

"Ah . . . Okay, but it's going to be hard to wait."

He left with a pout, and Janine thought he had acted that out pretty well.

"Hello! Is this Meghan? It's Grandma . . . Are you about to have dinner? We are wondering if you all might like to come over for dessert today. I have apple pies in the oven."

"Just a minute, Grandma."

"Hello, Mother. It's Kathy. You baked apple pies today?"

"Yes. Julia and I went to the orchard and bought bags of apples. Can you all come for dessert after supper?"

"The Chef says yes."

"Okay. It sounds like the challenge is on." She laughed. "Tell Greg to be ready for a delicious apple pie. His pie baking is stupendous, of course, but I'm confident today that I have found a secret to this apple pie business."

"Oh, good. This will be fun. We'll see you at six o'clock?"

"Perfect!"

The timer was going off. She opened the door to three beautiful pies and lifted the first one out, marveling at the perfection. The other two were just as beautiful. "By Jove, I believe I've done it!" Of course, *tasting* is believing, but she was not worried. She had mixed up the apples with the sugar, cinnamon, allspice, nutmeg, flour, and a little butter, put a half cup into a pan, and cooked it slightly just to be sure she had figured out the right amount of flavorings and thickening for the interesting combination of apples. *Yum, yum, Marcia was right! These apples combine together to make the perfect-tasting pie.*

John heard Prince coming. They had walked over—a good afternoon for it.

"I've been waiting for you. Come in and get a whiff of the pies." They all smiled and obliged. The fragrance permeated the house—a lovely bouquet of spice, fruit, and pastry. The Chef had his nose up and wiggling. He arrogantly followed the wafting fragrance and found himself in the kitchen whereupon he spied the source of this sultry beckoning. He slowly walked around the island where three tantalizing beauties were displayed in scintillatingly luscious coatings.

"Hmm . . . They certainly seem to be perfect, but beauty is only skin deep. With an apple pie, it's what's on the inside that counts. I insist that we conduct a deep and thorough examination before declaring the final results."

He was having a good time acting like the instructor at a Grand Gourmet Academy. "Who will serve?" he asked with eyebrows lifted and nose still pointed upward.

"Sir," answered Janine. "Please, sir, allow me."

"As you will."

"Will you all take a seat at the table? Sir Gregory, if you will please be seated at the head of the table?"

Naturally, she had a tablecloth on the table. There were pretty floral napkins and china dishes, glasses of ice water, and cups and saucers for coffee. Prince found his place under the middle of the table and prepared himself for the final pronouncement.

"Sir, would you care for ice cream with your slightly warm apple pie?"

"But of course!"

"And for our other guests?" She was being very prim and proper.

They all picked up their napkins and placed them on their laps and, following the lead of Chef Gregory, sat straight up and politely waited.

When all were served, they deferred to the Chef to take the first taste.

He cut a small bite of pie, dipped the pie and fork into the ice cream, lifted it to his pursed lips . . . He smelled it . . . looked at it carefully . . . and opened up his mouth as everyone's mouths were beginning to water. The pie was inside . . . Slowly, slowly he let it settle into his taste buds and chewed even more slowly. He swallowed.

Everyone in the room had taken on the role of spectator at a huge event. Chef Gregory looked at Janine. He nodded . . . Nothing more.

Not a fork had been lifted. They kept looking at Chef Gregory, waiting for his evaluation. He looked at Janine again—and smiled!

He stood and bowed to her. "Madam, this is the best apple pie I have ever tasted."

They all cheered and ran and hugged Janine. What a crazy bunch! Everyone was thinking the same thing.

Oh, yes. It was good all right. It was totally delicious.

Greg asked Janine what was her secret. Janine selfishly decided not to tell; however, she did send a pie home with the Langs and challenged them to analyze it and see if they could discover the secret ingredient. Chef Gregory was eager to accept. It was a jolly good time for the family—so different from any they had ever had before.

When everyone left, John and Janine had a good laugh about the "tasting," but John had to admit to Janine that the declaration was true. It was the best apple pie ever. They cleaned up the kitchen and went out onto the deck to watch the sunset together.

22

October Fest

Janine stepped outside that Saturday morning in October as a flock of geese flew over the house, bringing noisy news of the winter to come. The mornings were turning crisp, and she was thinking that she probably would not be sitting on the deck much longer. She would certainly miss her personal time with the birds, the rising sun, and a peaceful greeting from the Lord, but she would adjust to welcoming in the morning from indoors.

Today was October Fest in West Hope, and they would be going into town early. They were eager to see what an October Fest was. Kathy's family stopped by for them, and they arrived in West Hope at about ten o'clock.

"Oh my! Look at all of the cars here. I can't believe it!" Janine said.

"I know. That's why I told you to wear your walking shoes. We're going to have to go over to the park and walk from there. That's what Maggie told me. Turn here onto Mercy Street," Kathy said.

The ballpark was nearly full of cars. An elderly man was directing the cars for parking. There was no charge, just a smile and a "Good morning. Have a great day."

The little community was bustling with people and the sweet aroma of baking and cooking. Tables were set up on all the porches with some on the sidewalks. They decided they would not begin purchasing right away but should look around first.

They found tables with fudge, cupcakes, and all sorts of baked goods. Dishcloths, scarves, crocheted and knitted items, and many crafts were on display also. Children were running to and fro, having a good time of it as parents were calling to them to stay close. There was excitement in the air as the quiet little borough had become transformed into a lively, overpopulated street scene with people of all ages.

Before they moved along much farther, they could hear the sounds of a marching band coming up from behind. Everyone was moving aside and squeezing along the cobblestone sidewalks to make room for the parade. What a pleasant surprise!

They scooted into the tightly grouped crowd, smiling and clapping their hands as the band came by playing a Sousa march. In front of the band were majorettes twirling, flag bearers, and a sign stretched across the entire street with the name of a local high school across it.

It wasn't a large band, but they sure could play that music. Everyone was keeping time in one way or another, enjoying the revelry, the music, and the spirit of the band and the crowd.

Janine and John had not witnessed such an occasion before. They could only compare it with a college pep rally as though the school band was marching the students to a bonfire. They were caught up in the excitement as was everyone there.

Clowns joined in behind with many helium-filled balloons, passing them out to the children, free of cost. Behind the clowns were children on bicycles, each decorated in colorful crepe paper and other such decorations. Janine felt as though they had been transported into a lost time zone. Could this really be happening? Do other small communities have parades such as this? The Stephenses didn't know the answer but wouldn't have missed this precious moment for the world!

The parade wasn't very long, but it was perfect! Everyone was in a happy mood, almost dancing along from place to place. The Stephenses moved forward, all smiles, wondering what could top that for the day.

They came upon a couple, caning chairs. Janine had no idea what they were doing, and so she asked them about it.

"Mrs. Stephens, it's nice to see you here today," the lady said.

Janine cringed. She was trying to find comfort in the familiarity, but it still caused an uncomfortable anxiety within.

"Hello," she said. "How do you know who I am?"

"Oh, I see you in church. We've never met. I'm Emily Evans, and this is my husband, Walter. We've been caning chairs for a long time. Here, let me show you—"

It was a fascinating and very specialized art. Emily told her that she received requests from people to repair their antique chairs all the time and that she and her husband enjoyed working on the projects together.

Across the street was Julia's house. She wasn't on the porch, but Janine knew that she had baked her cookies and was planning to be out today. She suggested they go over and see if they could help her set up. Janine knocked on the door, and Julia answered immediately.

"Janine! So you've come to our Fest, have you? I hope you got to see the parade. Come on in."

"We did! This is just wonderful, Julia . . . We wondered if you needed some help carrying things outside this morning, or have you decided it's too cool to come out right now?"

"No, no. I'm ready. I'm a little slower than most, I suppose. But if you'd like to help, it would be fine. I need that table set up and the cloth put on it."

"Julia, this is Kathy and her husband, Greg, and their children, Karen and Meghan."

Julia beamed brightly. "It is wonderful to meet you, Kathy."

"Thank you, Julia. I'm happy to meet you. Mother speaks very highly of you."

Janine thought it was very special to have her family finally meet her newfound friend Julia. She spoke to the girls, "Would you please help to gather up some items for Mrs. Gillanders?"

They were delighted to help. John picked up the table and put it on the porch. The girls took out the boxes of cookies, and Kathy picked up Julia's chair. Soon everything was ready, and people were buying. They stayed with Julia for a while, and Anne came along with a tote bag full of something to set up on Julia's porch.

"Hello, Anne. Have you met the Stephenses?"

"Hello. I'm Anne Kendrick. It's nice to meet you. I've seen you in church. Julia and I have been friends for a long time."

"I'm Janine, and this is John. Our daughter Kathy and her family are with us today—Greg, Karen, and Meghan. Oh, you have beautiful little quilts here. Did you make them?"

"Yes, I've made a lot of quilts over the years but have given all of the standard-sized ones to my family and others. I still enjoy the workings of it all, so I made some small ones for the babies today."

Janine helped her set out the quilts on the porch banister, and they left the ladies to do what they had planned. Janine said she'd stop by again on the way back.

By the time they got to Iola's house, they were getting hungry and bought a dozen of her Monster Cookies. They were full of yummy candies, chocolate chips, nuts, and were very large, just as the name implied. The girls were ecstatic and ate one on the porch. What a cookie! They were perfect cookies for teenagers.

From Iola's porch, they could look down upon much of the community. They could have sat there all day, just observing the fun of it all.

Turning toward Janine, Iola asked, "Well, what do you think of our little community today?"

"I think it's delightful. Does everyone in the neighborhood get involved?"

"Pretty much so. It was a lot easier years ago when we were younger. I think this will be my last year."

"Well, these cookies are wonderful! Do you ever pass along the recipe?" asked Janine.

"I'll bring it to church tomorrow. I think most of the people around here have it, but they leave it to me to make them for the October Fest."

"Thank you very much. I think we'll go over to the church to have lunch. Can I bring something back to you?"

"No, no. I have everything I need here. Thanks for stopping by."

"You're welcome. We've enjoyed the visit." They excused themselves and turned toward the church.

Iola looked after them as they walked away. She had felt invigorated by their visit.

How nice, she thought. *Janine and I seemed to have mutual interests, and it was good to talk with someone who actually listened.*

It was frustrating to Iola that she had become one of the "old ladies." *We might as well be invisible. No one seems to think we have one word of value.*

Iola was upset with herself for thinking that way, yet she continued. *I try not to open my mouth anymore because no one listens or seems to care what I have to say. Being old doesn't mean we don't care. We'd all like to be useful in some way.*

Iola was one of the pillars of the church. She had served in many leadership positions, spending hours each week at the church or at home, planning ahead for meetings. Church attendance had declined over the years, which pained her considerably. Of course, most churches were experiencing the same thing, but Iola felt that was no excuse to stop trying. *We need new programs, and a little evangelism wouldn't hurt either. Well, it looks like we're going to have a new family in the church. New people bring new ideas.* She felt encouraged.

They climbed the hill to the church and went inside. The lunch was downstairs, and most of the tables there were full of happy people, talking and eating lunch together.

A sign was posted: "Apple Pie Bakeoff at the Orchard Restaurant—10:00 p.m."

Greg said, "Janine, you should have entered the contest."

Janine was pleased with him saying that. "Well, thank you very much. I wonder if they are selling those pies or what? I'd sure like to taste them, wouldn't you?"

"Madam, I have already tasted the best," he responded. Janine was bursting at the seams.

Pastor Daniel approached them and extended a sincere welcome. Janine and John introduced the members of their entourage as the pastor led them to a table to be seated. "You are going to enjoy the lunch as the church ladies are noted for their excellent soup making. Did you walk through the borough?"

"We did, but we need to go backtracking and see more of everything. I especially want to purchase one of those gorgeous grapevine wreathes and look over some of the other crafts. Julia Gillanders is selling orange cookies, and I hope they are not all sold out by the time we get back to her."

"Well, good luck on that. She's pretty famous for those cookies. No one else has the recipe, and everyone likes them."

One of the ladies from the church came over to get their orders. The pastor introduced Virginia Moen as one of the best cooks in the area.

"Now, now. Let's not try to fool these nice people. How are all of you today?"

"Great. It's nice to meet you, Virginia."

"We have chicken noodle, chili, and vegetable beef. Every bowl comes with homemade biscuits. Or if you'd prefer, we have sandwiches. Here's a menu of the sandwiches."

They studied the menu, and everyone ordered soup with biscuits, reserving room for one of the many desserts on the side table.

"This is nice," Kathy said.

"Yes. I have never been down here to the fellowship hall. Someone certainly knows how to decorate. It's beautiful . . . Kathy, you should come to church some Sunday. I think you would like the church service."

"I'm going to sometime soon. I've decided that I need to move on, and I hope that the members of the little church will realize that they have to too."

Francine Simmons stopped at their table to say hello, and Janine remembered her name and introduced her around. "Janine, could I have your telephone number? I'd like to ask a favor of you."

"Of course, Francine. Here. I'll give it to you."

"Thank you. I may call you later today. Would that be all right?"

"Yes, we'll be home."

"That's good. Thank you."

Janine wondered what the favor would be. She thought it would have something to do with the choir, but she had already said that she didn't think she'd want to participate in the choir at this time. Well, she'd not bother trying to figure that out now.

A few other parishioners stopped by. They finished a very nice lunch and set out to retrace their steps of the earlier part of the day, as it was too far to walk to the Orchard Restaurant to check out the pie bake-off. They came upon Bea Roberts's house. Another lady was on the porch with her, and they were laughing about something.

Noticing Janine and her family, they stood up and welcomed them. "Hello, Mrs. Stephens. Welcome to the Fest. Have you met Adele Marsh?"

Once again, introductions were held. After this day, Janine figured she knew everyone in the community. "Hello, Adele. Are you a part of that well-known Sunday school class too?"

"I guess I am. I live over across the street there."

"That's nice. What are you ladies selling today?"

"Bea makes the best peanut brittle there is. I just came over for a while to keep her company."

"Peanut brittle?" John asked. It was one of his favorite candies. He looked at Janine and smiled. "How much do you have?"

"Now, John. Don't get carried away. Look at all of the people who would miss out if you bought all she has."

"Well, I think he could have one of these little boxes, don't you, Mrs. Stephens?"

Janine smiled and said, "Sure. All good softball players need a little peanut brittle now and then."

There was music in the air—bagpipe music! The Stephens and family were drawn from the porch scene to discover the source of the glorious sound. They promptly asked the ladies about it.

"Oh, that's Mr. Gordon. He loves his bagpipe and so do we, so he's probably strutting up the street, charming the crowd with his music as he does each and every year," Bea said.

"Oh, let's go find him," said Meghan. They all enthusiastically agreed and off they went.

"Enjoy your day," called Adele. They assured them that they had already. The music of the piper was calling them, but they stopped at the porch where Janine had seen the grapevine wreathes. She was thrilled when she found the perfect one for the season to put on her front door.

Shortly afterward, carrying peanut brittle, a wreath, and bags of other goodies, they came upon a crowd in the middle of the street who had gathered to listen to Mr. Gordon playing a lilting "jig" of sorts. Children were dancing around to the music while the adults were tapping their toes and clapping along. And what a spectacle Mr. Gordon was, and very handsome! He had cherry-red cheeks with sparkling eyes, obviously enjoying himself as much as the crowd, and was dressed from head to toe in Scottish array.

His kilt was of green and blue plaid, and he had socks to his knees, a cap on his head, a scarf, tie, and many ornamentations. No one in the Stephens family was expecting to see and hear from a piper today, and this interlude crowned the day with blissful amazement.

They joined the crowd and listened awhile until Mr. Gordon began walking up the street again playing "Loch Lomond" by request.

They linked arms, practically skipping along and laughing. They eventually arrived at Julia's porch again. There were Julia and Anne sitting and looking rather tired. Everything from the porch was gone! "Julia, I hope you enjoyed your day," Janine said.

"Oh, we did. We saw so many people we know and haven't seen for such a long time. I think we did more talking than anything, don't you, Anne?"

"Yes, it was a nice day, but I'm going to have to go pick up Owen and get us back to the apartment. Julia, I enjoyed being with you today. I hope you aren't too tired."

"No, Anne, I'm fine. I'll see you tomorrow."

"Did you sell all of your cookies, Julia?" Janine asked.

"I did! They were gone in no time, but I put a dozen of them aside and saved them for you."

"Well, how wonderful of you, Julia. Thank you so much." Julia didn't want to take John's money, but he insisted.

"It's been a really fun day, Julia. I wonder how many people passed through here."

"Well, last year, they said there were about two thousand people here in that one day, and I think we've had about the same again. It's good for the community, but tough on us old gals. Oh, I don't know, I suppose it's all a good idea. Most of the people who come want to be back next year, and everyone seems to think we have a special kind of town here. 'Quaint' they say. Maybe so. It's just home to us."

John asked if they could do anything for her, and Julia said she was fine. She planned to go put her feet up for a while. The Stephens family went to the car and home, remarking about the "quaint" day it actually was, like going back in time somehow. They were happy and sang old-time songs and a couple of Scottish tunes all the way home.

ϒϒϒ

John and Janine were hanging the new wreath onto the front door when the telephone rang. "I'll get it, John."

"Hello."

"Hello, Mrs. Stephens. This is Francine Simmons."

"Oh, yes."

"Did you enjoy the October Fest?"

"We all did. I was shocked to see how many people were in West Hope. How do they know about the event?"

"It's advertised in the newspapers, and since it has been an annual event for quite some time, many of the same people return for the day and ofttimes bring others along. We are always amazed at the turnout too. But it gives us all something to look forward to and to plan for . . . As I said this afternoon, I have a favor to ask of you."

"Yes?"

"Well, my husband and I had been hoping to go visit his mother in Florida for the Christmas holidays, and Lawrence's house there needs some attention and fixing up. I was wondering if you would kindly fill in for me at the organ for a few weeks?"

Uh-oh! Now what am I supposed to do?

"Uh, Francine, I really don't know what to say. I don't believe I'm ready to actually take on any responsibility in the church. At least not yet."

"I realize this is sudden for you. I wouldn't be asking except that Lawrence and I had made a promise to his mother that we would do everything we could to arrange to get down there this year. It's so hard to find someone to play the organ, especially at a small church."

"I do understand, Francine, and I'll think and pray about it and give you an answer soon, if that's all right."

"Oh, yes. Thank you. I would appreciate it very much if you would do that. Let me know whenever you have reached a decision. You wouldn't have to direct the choir. They are used to singing without direction. Well, anyway, thanks again."

"You're welcome. I'll be in touch."

She walked outside where John was standing away from the house, tilting his head and looking at the front door.

"Is it straight?"

She moved alongside him. It was fine except he had hung it upside down. *How on earth could he do that? Didn't I have a hook?*

"John, it's upside down."

"What? I think that's the way it's supposed to be."

"No. Wait a minute." She went to the door, took down the wreath, and found the hook on the bottom. "John, come look."

He walked over and saw what she meant by the hook. "I thought you could just catch any of the vines on a nail. Sorry."

"That's okay . . . There. How does that look now?"

"Good . . . Very nice." She stood over beside him. It did look nice . . . Homey, one could say.

"Guess who called."

"Who?"

"Francine Simmons, the church organist."

"Yes, I know who she is. What did she want?"

"She asked me to fill in on the organ while she and Lawrence go to Florida over the Christmas holidays to visit his mother . . . Don't say anything. I don't want to talk about it right now. I need to pray about it."

"I understand . . . Okay."

Janine felt somewhat disturbed over the request and decided not to think anymore about it today. She would simply continue to reflect upon the surprisingly wonderful day they all had at the October Fest.

23

Francine's Hope

"Lawrence, Janine is the last resort, but she didn't give me an affirmative answer. We'll have to wait for her to think about it." Francine seemed worried. After all, she had called every lead given to her, and no one was available during the holidays. It would help if only someone in the church could play the piano.

"Well, don't give up hope, Fran. We'll do what we must. If we are supposed to go, it will work out."

"Thank you, Lawrence. You are my encourager. Janine didn't say no, so maybe she'll actually say yes."

"That's my girl. Come. Sit over here with me. We've had a busy day."

She sat beside him on the sofa, he put his arm around her, and she rested her head upon his chest. She felt comfort in him and drifted into a quiet nap.

The Sunday morning devotion for Janine was based upon Galatians 6. Paul instructed Christians to not live independently but to work together for the common good. "Carry each other's burdens, and in this way you will fulfill the law of Christ." She thought of Francine and her need to fulfill a promise—an important one for herself and her husband. Fran was carrying a burden in a manner of speaking as she felt strongly the need to stay at Hope Church unless someone would minister through the music for her.

God was speaking to Janine through His word this morning, and it became clearer as to what she should do with Francine's request as she read on to the tenth verse of the chapter:

Therefore, as we have opportunity *(opportunity!)*, let us do good to all people, especially to those who belong to the family of believers.

That is clear enough for me! I can "do good" for my sister in Christ and carry on the work she does in the church while she is visiting her mother-in-law. Thank You, Lord, for giving me the direction and helping me to make a right decision. I'll speak to Francine about this today.

Janine told John of her decision, and he felt it was the right thing to do. They moved along with getting ready for church and, even though they seemed to be on time, found themselves arriving just as the service was about to begin. They scurried to their normal pew, smiled at Julia, who was sitting alone this morning, and turned their attention to the worship of the Lord.

"Julia, is Jenny ill?" Janine asked following the service.

"Sometimes she has more trouble with her back than usual and then it's hard to drive the miles to and from church."

"We could have sat together this morning. I was late in getting here or we would have invited you to sit with us. Would you want to do that on days that Jenny cannot get here?"

"Yes, I would. I'll move down on those Sundays. Thanks."

"Are you rested from yesterday?"

"Not entirely. I'll be fine though and will try to get some practicing in before Tuesday."

Janine smiled. "I'll look forward to it."

Francine came by and stood silently until Julia moved over to her Sunday school friends. "Good morning, Janine."

"Good morning, Francine. I've come to a decision about your request. Could we find a place to sit and talk for a few minutes?"

Francine was nervous but needed to know the answer nevertheless. "Let's go into the classroom over there," she suggested.

"John, I'll be along shortly."

He nodded and began a conversation with Raymond.

The two sat at a table surrounded by chairs. Francine waited for Janine to begin.

"I believe the Lord wants me to do what I can to help my sister in the faith, so I will gladly fill in for you while you take a leave to visit your mother-in-law."

"Oh, thank you so much! Lawrence will be very happy too."

"When do you plan to go?"

"We thought we'd leave on the tenth of December and return around the third or fourth of January. Does this seem to be okay with you?"

"Yes, of course. I'll be here. Do you have choir practices scheduled?"

"If you'd like to come to work with the choir and myself on the first and second Tuesdays of the month, that would be just wonderful, and then you can get a feel for the anthems we've planned."

"That's fine. Will there be a Christmas Eve service?"

"Yes. Would you be able to be here for that?"

"I had thought about going to my home church for Christmas Eve to visit with some of my old friends who always return for that, but if there is a service here at Hope Church, I'll plan to be here."

"Janine, I don't know how to express my gratitude to you."

"The Lord wants you to go, and He has placed me here to help . . . It's part of His Plan, I'm sure, so don't thank me—thank Him."

"Oh, I will . . . I do! Believe me!"

ϒϒϒ

When piano lessons were finished on Tuesday, Janine was eager to talk with Julia.

"Julia, I wonder if you might tell me about Francine. I know she was married a short time ago. Was this her first marriage?"

"Yes, she's one of the nicest women, and yet it seemed forever before some nice man realized that."

"Would you believe that we saw the church sign with the wedding congratulations last year? We noticed it as we were driving through to go to Kathy's one Sunday."

"That was a wonderful day, Janine. The entire congregation stayed after church. Everyone was so happy for Francine, and Lawrence too. Francine had been a member here all of her life. Her husband just started coming here the year before, and they met and fell in love. We all say it was meant to be."

"I'm sure! Well, anyway, Francine has asked me to play the organ during the Christmas holidays while she and Lawrence go to visit Lawrence's mother."

"Are you going to do it?"

"Yes."

"How about that? I'm going to tell you something that you won't hardly believe!"

"What?" Her curiosity was peaked.

"When Francine and Lawrence got married, Fran asked the officers of the church to try to find someone to replace her if possible so that she and Lawrence could spend at least half of the year in Florida. Well, that was a year ago. I understand that they have been praying ever since, and nothing has happened.

But when the official board decides to pray, they don't stop because their prayers haven't been answered right away. So as far as I know, they are still praying."

"So, you think I came here in answer to their prayers?"

"Well, I really can't say for sure. Anyway . . . what do you think?"

"She only asked me to play for about four weeks."

"I know."

Neither of them could talk about it for a while as they were both assessing the situation.

Does God really answer a prayer like that? Julia was wondering.

Lord, I need to talk with You, Janine prayed silently.

"Julia, I have some things I need to do, so I'd better hurry along. I'm sorry to rush out like this."

"Oh, that's fine. You go ahead. We've had a good day, even if I wasn't very well prepared. But I promise to do better next week."

"Julia, I'm extremely proud of you as it is. You are amazing. Everyone has a busy week at times, so please don't worry about having to repeat a couple of pieces. You like them anyway and will enjoy playing them a week longer, I think."

"You're right. I love that 'Sorrento' song. It reminds me so much of the Italians who lived right next to us when I was a child. They were such happy people, and they would get together on their porch in the evenings and sing. One of them played an accordion. That was one of their songs. I can't believe that I am playing it now."

"How nice. Well, you enjoy the music. I'll have to start practicing too. I'm sure to be pretty rusty these days. You know what they say: 'Use it or lost it' . . . It's the truth."

ʏʏʏ

Janine drove into the garage, went rushing into the house, jumped into her walking shoes and sweatpants, and told John she was going to walk awhile.

John had seen her scurrying around and now knew that she had something strongly on her mind. He smiled and nodded—that was it.

She went out the door, leaving a breeze in her wake.

She turned to the left and was almost jogging as she was eager to get going.

Lord, my Lord, did you bring me here to minister through music? I have been holding back because I didn't want to interfere with Your Plan for me. Francine has only asked for four weeks.

She kept walking very fast as though she would get an answer faster that way. But none came . . . She slowed down and realized that she wasn't really listening—just venting. Where was her patience and how could she find the answer if she didn't listen?

Father in heaven, I am Your servant. I will do whatever you ask of me because I know that You love me. I know that You love Your children of West Hope. Help me to understand my calling here. I know I am in the right place. I'm very sure of that. I also believe that Julia needs me and I'm supposed to be with her right now . . . I'm not sure why . . . I think it's because You love her so much that You have provided a means for her happiness.

What else should I be doing? I certainly have more time than Julia requires. Is it the church music?

Questions—no answers.

Is it coincidence that she is in the right place at the right time?

Francine's life changed . . . Then Janine's life changed . . . Coincidence? No!

If this is an act of God, then He really loves Francine. He has moved "mountains" to answer her prayer. I can understand that. Fran has been a faithful servant all of her life.

"God so loved the world—"

God still loves the world.

Janine was analyzing everything. Well, it could, couldn't it? She was not absolutely sure.

I'll keep praying about it. In the meantime, I will be serving as organist for a few weeks. The Lord will surely reveal His purpose to me.

She looked up from her contemplative state of mind and discovered that she was in the vicinity of the Detelle's. *My goodness, I'd better turn around and get home.* As Tony turned into his driveway, he noticed Janine walking. He pulled over alongside of her and offered to give her a ride back home.

"Thank you, Tony, but I'm exercising. I need to do more of it."

He smiled and went on home.

Yes, I do need to do more of this. I fear that I have been drifting lately.

When she got home, John was waiting for her. "Hi, honey. I made a fresh pot of coffee. Come on and have a cup."

"Thanks. That sounds good."

They sat and ate some of Julia's delicious orange cookies and talked about the events of Janine's day. They were both perplexed.

John said, "Someday we'll have the answer, whether in this world or the next."

24

Wintering

Winter was upon the community of West Hope and the entire eastern portion of the United States. John never did get all his leaves into the woods, but he was told that the Lord would see to it with a mighty wind in November, and that's exactly what happened.

The Stephenses were not used to hearing the howling of the winds, having lived between houses in the city for all their years together. This new experience was somewhat unnerving to Janine, but John assured her that it would take a big, big wolf to blow their brick home.

"If only it would snow," Janine said day after day. She had been getting up every morning, looking out of the windows, hoping to see her rural home in a serene, snow-covered setting. All she found were small branches blown down from the night before in a bleak and unrelenting cold gloom.

The ladies of West Hope were entering their most difficult months of the year—months pretty much alone except for the telephone, radio, and television. Julia was more grateful than ever to have Janine teaching her piano. They would spend a couple of hours each visit, and she realized she was luckier than most.

The adult Sunday school classes were as empty as were the lives of those who belonged to them. The choir members were faithful, believing that they had a calling to be in church and assist with the worship every Sunday. They were still meeting on Tuesday evenings for practice and would do so until it began to snow. Winters here in these hills could be brutal, and most of the people who didn't have day jobs just hunkered in for the long winter's run.

Janine enjoyed getting acquainted with the choir, and they worked well together. Francine was gone now, and Janine was on her own. It was no problem for her. She had spent a major portion of her adult life with church music.

Along about the second week of December, Julia developed a cough and couldn't have Janine come for a lesson. Janine insisted on stopping by and was shocked to see Julia looking so poorly. She found her curled up in her chair with blankets and tissues, feeling hot to the touch and hadn't seen a doctor.

"Do you have Dr. McHenry's telephone number, Julia? I think I should call him."

"Now, Janine, it's just a cold. I'll be all right."

"Julia, please, I'm worried about you. Please let me call him."

The telephone number was scribbled inside of the phone book, and Julia told her to go ahead and make the call.

Here in this little town, everyone called upon Dr. McHenry for everything—from broken fingers to fever and chest congestion. Janine had met him before and realized that he was an essential person in the community. He kept an office in his home at the west end of town, and had been here since he was a young man and married a local girl. Like most of the others, he came and he stayed.

"Dr. McHenry, this is Janine Stephens."

"Oh, yes, Mrs. Stephens. What can I do for you?"

She told him of her findings with Julia, and he decided to stop over during his lunch hour to check on her. Janine would be staying with her until then, she told him. He arrived around 12:20 p.m. and soon made a diagnosis.

"Ms. Julia, you do not have pneumonia yet, so we are good there. Are you drinking plenty of water?"

"Well, I try to."

"Tryin's not good enough. I want you to fill three quart jars with water every morning and drink it all by nighttime. I also want you to drink orange juice, eat some broth with bread in it, take an extra aspirin every four hours. You also must rest, lying down, in bed or a makeshift bed in the morning, in the afternoon, and early evening."

He told Janine he would call in a prescription for her, and the pharmacist would deliver it today. The medicine would help relieve the congestion to lessen the possibility of pneumonia. Apparently, Julia had pneumonia before, and he was concerned about that.

Janine had never heard of prescription delivery. Apparently, there was a nice drugstore near the outskirts of Innesport that always looked out for the folks in the nearby small towns.

When he left, she shook her head in amazement. Is this actually the end of the twentieth century, or was she dreaming? She had just witnessed the loving kindness of a house-calling doctor and learned of a pharmacy that would deliver. Her old friends would not believe her if she told this little story; however, that wasn't important at the moment. She wanted Julia to get better, so she would do her part.

Before she left for the general store, she pulled out some bedding for Julia and prepared a comfortable place for her to rest on the sofa. Janine said that she would warm up some broth when she returned.

Elda was distressed to learn of Julia's illness. They gathered up the items, and Elda said she would check in on Julia in the early evening.

A few snowflakes began to fall as she returned to Julia's, but she was too concerned about Julia's health to even notice. During the next hour, she saw to it that there was water handy and that Julia had eaten at least part of the bowl of broth and bread. She put the orange juice in the refrigerator, and Julia assured her that she would drink some after resting awhile.

Janine is so kind to me. I wonder why. I'm just an old lady, trying to learn something new. There's nothing special about me that should draw her to me. Well, I'm not going to try to figure it out . . . I guess I couldn't anyway. I'm sure happy she has come today. It feels warm and comfortable in these blankets. Maybe I can sleep.

Janine left West Hope after going across the street to the neighbors who were always looking in on Julia. She told them of her condition, and they would be stopping over occasionally to be with her. She gave them her telephone number, and they said they would call if necessary. Of course, Dr. McHenry had said the same thing, so Janine felt that Julia would be watched after.

It was snowing a lot more now. She didn't know if there was a winter storm warning, so she headed for home. Well, warning or not, here it came—the snow she had wanted! By the time she was home, the biggest flakes she had ever seen covered the roads, and it didn't appear the snow would be stopping soon.

When she pulled into her driveway, she saw her home sitting in a perfect, picture-card setting. "John. John. Get the camera!" she said.

He gave it to her, and she convinced him to come outside while she took his picture in the snow. It was glorious! The trees! The trees! The branches were laden in fluffy white snow, and the cardinals were flying around the feeder. If she could capture a picture of a cardinal in the snow in her front yard, she would use it for a Christmas card.

John and Janine were as excited as children. They decided to put on boots, hats, and gloves, and take a winter walk. "Let it snow, let it snow, let it snow," they sang as they walked along arm-in-arm, covered from falling snow from head to toe and looking like two dancing snowmen. They went inside holding hands, cherry-cheeked, and ready for hot chocolate.

The granddaughters and Prince came bounding over later in the afternoon, and the girls built two splendid snowmen for them in the front yard. John gathered up some sticks, Janine added carrot noses and found two old hats to put on their heads—one for the elegant lady and one for the gentleman. Janine canceled choir practice, which was handled very efficiently by the telephone "tree" established within the choir, and invited the girls to stay for supper.

It was a beautiful time, and when the girls came in, John had the fire going in the living room. They all entered by the downstairs to get out of the now-wet clothes. They laughed at putting on Grandma's sweatpants while their outerwear was being dried in the clothes dryer. John gave Prince a good rubdown. He was totally compliant, loving every minute of it, and then they scampered upstairs to the warm, warm fireplace.

Janine was blissful with the first snow, the warm and cozy home, and the opportunity to have the girls join them for the evening. She asked them if they'd like to spend the night since school was canceled for the next day, and they jumped at the idea! Everything was quickly arranged and produced moments to remember for all of them.

John was always happy to have his girls around. He loved playing board games with them, and they sat in front of the fireplace for quite some time, trying to outdo one another. When they were all tucked in and Prince was beside the bed, they said prayers of thankfulness with Grandma for the special day and for being together.

Janine had earlier telephoned Julia, who answered right away.

"Julia, this is Janine. I've been thinking about you. Are you getting along all right?"

"Yes, thank you, and thank you too for all of your help this morning. I'm going to stay downstairs tonight on this cozy bed you made up for me. That'll save me climbing the steps. You must have talked with some people in town because Elda stopped by and so did Emily from across the street. They each took care of getting me some broth or juice. I have plenty of water."

"Thank goodness. I was worried that I wouldn't be able to get back to see you with all of the snow."

"Don't worry. They both will be back, and the pharmacist brought me some medicine. I'll be fine. I've been alone a long time, Janine. We learn to do what we must."

"All right. I'll call you again tomorrow. I hope you'll be better tomorrow. Take care of yourself. Good night."

"Thank you. Good night."

The phone call helped each of them to feel better. Janine could get back to relaxing and enjoying her first winter's night in her new home with complete peace of mind.

25

Home for the Holidays

Janine was fulfilling her organ duties at church without any difficulty, never knowing for sure if playing the organ was part of the Plan. However, she couldn't see any reason why she shouldn't be helping, and it certainly was a good thing for Francine. She relaxed into the flow of it and concentrated on preparing her home for Christmas.

They would have a "live" Christmas tree—something they hadn't done in years! Actually, John found a tree farm not far from their home and had marked a tree for cutting himself. He would bring it home the week before Christmas. They couldn't stop decorating. Janine had collected so many whatnots over the years, and naturally, she had an entire set of Christmas dishes. She took them out of the cartons and moved them into the kitchen cupboards so they could use them every day.

John brought yards of pine from the woods, and they tied them together into garlands for outdoor trimming. The pine scent was intoxicating, and they could hardly wait to put the natural Christmas tree in front of the large living room window.

Janine was also enjoying the way the church was decorated. It was all natural: nothing fancy but simply beautiful. Angels graced the sanctuary from the top of every stained-glass window, and pine was placed in every window, tied in the center with a beautiful ribbon. The Sunday school children, with their darling, one-of-a-kind ornaments, lovingly decorated the Christmas tree. Janine took it upon herself to sing carols with them and enjoyed the occasion as much as anybody.

She was quite relieved that Julia improved daily from her cold but regretted that she and most of the ladies had not been out to church during the Advent season at all this year due to the snow and the bitterly cold weather. The ladies were saddened also, but they had become accustomed to missing out on many things as their years tallied up.

On Christmas Eve, the church filled up with families coming home. She was amazed at the crowd even though Julia had told her that "around here" everyone comes to church when they come to town. It had been true for Thanksgiving and now for Christmas. It was a beautiful seven o'clock service, early enough for the children to attend. Both of her daughters and their families came to be with Mom and Dad for the evening service, and Janine felt very much in her element at the organ. She overflowed with joy at celebrating the birth of Christ with her family. She resolved that she was doing what she was supposed to be doing because it felt so right.

The family all settled in at the new home after church. Kathy sat down at the piano to lead in the singing of carols.

Karen and Meghan sang "Away in a Manger" as a duet, which was appreciated by everyone.

The snow was falling softly outside, and Kathy pulled out the perfect piece for them: "The Snow Lay on the Ground," which continues "the stars shown bright, when Christ our Lord was born on Christmas night. *Venite adoremus.*"

Finally, to the delight of the girls, Greg handed the book *'Twas the Night before Christmas* to John and asked him if he would like to read the story this year.

John was very happy to do so as it had always been his practice to read this story to his own children. The girls sat at his feet attentively: Deborah snuggling up close to her daddy on his left and Kathy did the same on his right. They were as eager to hear the story once again as anyone.

"'Twas the night before Christmas when all through the house, not a creature was stirring, not even a mouse."

Deborah was so overjoyed that she could hardly hold back the tears, and Kathy was thankful to be there to hear her Daddy reading the story once again also.

Deborah and Robert were spending the night, and Kathy's family went on home to wait for Santa even though those days were long gone in actuality. They would be together tomorrow for a Christmas celebration and dinner prepared by the Chef.

When everything was quiet, Deborah confessed to her parents that she had been nervous about coming home for Christmas to a different home. She feared it just couldn't be the same. "But it is! It is even better somehow! You two seem to be so happy here, and it flows over into the entire family . . .

And you know what? I think this house must have been built for you to live in. It fits. Can you understand what I mean?"

They agreed with her. They were destined to be in this house for sure.

It was a fine Christmas for the Stephens family and would have been better if Harry, Rhonda, and the boys could have been with them this year. But Harry had a load of responsibilities at work, so he and Rhonda and the boys planned for many fun days at the ranch and local community. They would be together during the upcoming year, one way or another.

26

The "Call"

Francine returned to her responsibilities at the church, thankful for the time to visit with Lawrence's mother and furnish the home Lawrence had built. She still had hope that someone would soon be coming to take over her position at the church. She and Lawrence were eager to begin the life they presently had on hold. She called the chairman of the worship committee, Samuel Morris, to remind the committee once again that she appreciated their efforts to locate a replacement for her. She and Lawrence had decided that they would always try to be in Pennsylvania during the warm summer months, so perhaps the official board could search for someone to cover the months of October through May.

Samuel assured Francine that they were going to continue their search. They planned to ask Janine Stephens. She had seemed pleased to provide the music while Francine was vacationing.

"Lawrence, I know that very soon we will be returning to Florida. The committee is going to ask Janine to step into the position, at least for the winter months. Janine had said before that she felt she was here to help. I think everything is moving in that direction . . . I hope."

$$\Upsilon\,\Upsilon\,\Upsilon$$

"Hello!" Janine was answering a call.

"Mrs. Stephens, this is Samuel Morris of Hope Church. I'm the present chairman of the worship committee. I want to thank you for your wonderful contribution to our Advent and Christmas services while Francine was away."

"You're very welcome. It was my pleasure."

"The pastor and I wondered if you might have some time available to have a little talk with us concerning the music at the church."

"I could arrange time for that of course."

"Would you like to come to the church office? We could come to your home if you would prefer."

"I would enjoy having you come here. Reverend Daniel has wanted to visit anyway."

"Great. When would it be convenient?"

"You could come by today if you'd like. John and I aren't busy at all."

"Well, let me ask Reverend Daniel. I'm here at the church office . . . It's two o'clock right now. We could come by around two thirty. Would that be all right?"

"Yes, that would be just fine. We'll put the coffee pot on. Do you drink coffee?"

"Yes, Dan and I would both like that, so we'll be seeing you soon."

She hung up the phone and said, "John, something's up. That was the chairman of the worship committee at Hope Church, wanting to speak to me."

"Um-hm."

"What?"

"He's probably going to tell you what a fine job you did for them over the holidays and offer you a job."

"John, you know that's not so. Anyway, he already did say he appreciated the music I played. Maybe it has to do with the choir. I am going to sing with them, as we already decided. Or maybe he has in mind to have a children's choir. They do need one. I can't imagine a church without children singing."

"Well, when are they coming?"

She looked at her watch. "Oh, dear . . . very soon! I'm going to go freshen up a little. Would you start the coffee and set out four cups and saucers on the kitchen table for us?"

"Sure, you go ahead."

The guests were on time. Pastor Dan introduced Samuel to Janine and John, and they remembered him from church. They went on into the kitchen for the hot coffee that was promised. John sat with them for a short while and found a good reason to excuse himself.

Samuel spoke right. "Janine, perhaps you have already heard that Francine Simmons wants to move on to Florida as their permanent home and come this way for long visits."

Janine nodded, and he continued. "As much as we would miss Francine, we earnestly want her to be able to get on with this new and wonderful life God has given to her. However, she will not leave until another capable musician can come and replace her services here. We have searched for that person and haven't been able to find her until now."

Janine smiled. "That's wonderful. I'm sure Francine is very happy, and Lawrence also."

"Well, they will be when we get around to finalizing this, I'm sure. But for now there are still some things to settle."

"Oh, sorry. I guess I jumped ahead of you there . . . Please go on."

Samuel and Pastor Daniel looked at each other, trying to decide who would speak next. Finally, the pastor spoke up, "Janine, we believe that we've been led to ask you to come be our organist."

Janine just sat there. She should have known he was going to say that. John had even hinted at it earlier.

"You say you were led to ask me. How did you determine that?"

"We have been praying since the marriage for God to send us an organist . . . and now, Janine, you are here."

Janine almost fell over when he said those same words that she heard from God the very first day she went to Hope Church: "You are here."

Her heart seemed to stop, her arms felt numb, and her eyes were welling with tears. *Come on, Janine, they have only asked you to do a simple thing. Something you've done most of your life. Didn't you know this was coming? Why are you so shaken by thing?*

The pastor and Samuel recognized that Janine was upset. They didn't expect this reaction. She looked as though she was going to cry.

Janine did not realize that she was causing such concern. Time stood still, so she didn't even know that she had sat there for several minutes, not uttering a sound or even indicating that she heard them at all. She was motionless.

Finally, Reverend Daniel stood up and was about to express his apologies to Janine, but she stood also and asked him to please be seated.

"Please . . . I need a moment . . . Would you wait here while I ask John to join us?"

"Yes, of course," Samuel said. He wanted to say more but couldn't.

The men were extremely uncomfortable. They never expected anything more than a yes or no today. *Where did things take a turn? What is this all about?*

The Stephenses were back. John refreshed everyone's coffee, and as soon as all were seated, Janine told them her story. As she was telling it, it was obvious to the four of them that it was very significant to her and also to them.

Janine finished by telling them that she believed God dearly loves each and every one of His children. What He has done in this very small event in all history and even in this little community has given her joy and peace and a renewed understanding of all that God will do to provide for His children.

"Gentlemen, I thought I had everything under control in my world. I never considered changing. I was not truly close to the Lord, but I knew that He expected me to do good works for Him. So I busied and covered myself with "doing" as much as I possibly could do. My life was full of stress, and I would not stop long enough to listen to His calling or directions for my life. I give Him praise every day for lifting me from that foolishness and loving me enough to grace me with many wonderful changes. I had no idea that I could find such perfect peace in simply listening to His voice. I praise Him for leading me to a completely different life so that we can enjoy Him in this new and beautiful way. John and I are both happier than we have ever been. If we had stayed in the home at Innesport, we would have missed so much."

John jumped into her conversation. "She's right. We have both benefited from God's calling. I will be forever thankful for His loving kindness . . . and to Janine for willingly accepting His bidding."

"It wasn't me alone. It was John's support and understanding that kept me on track many times. But you've heard enough of this story. The answer to your question is yes. I already told Francine last November that I felt it was the Lord's will that I carry her burden for the holiday. Wait a minute! Did you even ask a question?"

They all laughed. There had *not* been a question.

Samuel asked, "Janine, would you be the organist at Hope Church for the months of October through May each year? Francine plans to be back here during the summer months and would be happy to share in the responsibility then."

That seemed so perfect! She and John had high hopes for taking a few trips now that she was not working so much. And if Francine would do that, they could plan their summers in an entirely different way. What could be better?

"John, what do you think?"

"I say, 'grab the iron while it's hot.'"

That brought a smile to everyone, and before the gentlemen left, it was settled. The men could hardly wait to tell Francine. Janine would love to be a little fly on the wall and see Francine's face and witness her excitement at the news. She was so happy knowing the joy this would bring to a beautiful couple that certainly deserved the benefits prepared for them.

Pastor Daniel led them in prayer: "Lord God, we know that 'all things work for good to those that love You and trust in You.' We thank You that Your servants, Janine and John, have put their total trust in You so that they may fulfill their roles in Your Kingdom as You have willed . . . and in so doing, Lord, are finding more happiness than they have ever known. We pray, Lord, that Your love will continue to envelop them and that Your light will shine upon them and upon the members of Hope Church so that together, we may live in Your favor and delight in carrying Your love and light into the world.

"Great God of Hope, we pray for our sister, Francine who has trusted in You completely to bring her to this day. Her hope has been realized, her prayers answered, and Your love demonstrated. May she and Lawrence live many years together in Your joy, Your peace, and Your protection.

"Be with us and help us, Lord, to never forget Your faithfulness to us and Your willingness to answer even the smallest of requests. We know, Lord, that in the entire universe, we are but a tiny speck, and yet even before the foundation of the world was begun, You knew us and will know us forever. We pray that You will be with us throughout our days in this world and that we will be with You in the world to come.

"We pray in the name of Jesus, our Savior and Friend . . . Amen."

The preacher seemed to have been unable to say enough, and those who were praying along with him felt the presence of the Lord. They were not eager to let go either.

ᴕᴕᴕ

Francine also received a call. "Hello!"

It was Samuel. "Francine, I have good news. On this day, your prayers have been answered. Janine Stephens has happily agreed to join with us at the Church of Hope as organist while you and Lawrence are in Florida from October through May each year."

"Oh, Samuel, thank you. And thanks be to God. This is wonderful news."

She hung up the phone, turned to Lawrence, and before she could say anything, he said with a wide smile and gleaming eyes, "I knew it!"

They hastened their plans and, before long, were off to fulfill their dreams. Janine was filled with joy and peace as she entered willingly into service at the church.

27

Another Long, Bleak Winter

Winter held on with record cold. Julia felt well enough to resume her piano practicing. *I think Janine can start coming by again if she wants to, and I can have another lesson. I need to practice and loosen up my fingers again.*

Unfortunately, the other ladies did not have the privilege of having someone come by to lift their spirits. They could only wait out the winter and hope to get to church soon. Pastor Dan called on each and every one of them often.

Rachael had come home from the hospital before Christmas only to find herself closed in a house alone most of the time. Her days were spent counting the days until the therapist would return. Of course, her son stopped in every day. *What would I do without Albert? I had thought my friends would be coming to visit, and now just see what's happening. No one can actually get here, except the therapist with her four-wheel auto, and the preacher who enjoys walking in the snow. I will be so happy to see spring arrive. This is enough to drive a person crazy!* She continued to work hard at walking with her walker, praying that the day would soon come when she could once again stand on her own two feet.

The second week of March brought violent winds, but behind that, the sun came out, bringing with it hope for better days ahead. The snow began to melt off, and soon, the ladies were venturing out and making arrangements to go to church again.

Janine suffered for them all. She knew through Julia that they needed one another, and they needed some kind of fun and enjoyment in their lives. She wished she knew what she might do. She found Julia's friends to be beautiful people—giving, caring, and now in their later years, lonely. She thought of them all the time.

Lord, is there something I can do to bring some joy into their lives?

28

Renewal

"John, come and see!"

"What's up, hon?"

"The crocuses! Look! They've popped through. Soon the daffodils will be out of the ground. I'm so happy that we decided to put some bulbs in last fall. Spring is finally coming."

"Um-hm. Have you seen a robin yet?"

"I haven't, but I heard one the other morning. This warmer weather means I'll be cutting grass again soon. I'm going to recondition the lawn mower, and I've been wondering if we should put in a little garden?"

"Oh John, you would love that. Of course you should . . . What will you plant?"

"Tomatoes for sure . . . and green peppers . . . a little lettuce on the outer edge . . . maybe a row or two of corn in the back rows."

"Hmm . . . how about zucchini? You love a zucchini casserole, and I could make sweet breads with them."

"That sounds terrific, but we'd need a large space for them. They vine out a lot."

"Your family always had a garden when you were young. I'm sure you could plan it well. Let's do it! Where?"

"First of all, we'd probably have to fence it in. I hear that the deer will eat up a garden around here. Would that bother you to have a fenced-in garden on this property?"

"Well, no, if we can put it down back a ways."

"We can do that as long as we fence it in, I should think."

"Well, you study it out, get your seeds or plants, or whatever. I love the idea!"

John was elated, and Janine loved seeing him this way. The initiative of planting a garden on their property gave permanency to their move.

ϒϒϒ

The ladies of West Hope were also seeing signs of spring. Julia's tiny white snow flowers were blooming; Iola was picking up fallen twigs a few at a time; Adele had seen a robin, and her daffodils were pushing through the ground next to the warmth of the house. Bea was walking around her driveway, searching for the first sign of her yellow irises; Laura was working very hard with her sons as the cows were calving. Anne noticed the warmth of the days as she went out for her daily walks; Rachael enjoyed listening to Albert talk about the plowing. Harriet chased after her puppy, which was now nearly a year old, and all were able to get back to Sunday school and church once again each week.

Alice Cook rarely had a ride to Sunday school since her daughter, Francine, had gone to Florida; however, when Jenny's back wasn't aching too badly, she always called Alice to go to church with her. Sunday was the best day of the week for the ladies.

ᐱᐱᐱ

Janine stopped into the ladies' class as she was on her way to her own class. They were all abuzz with conversation. She greatly enjoyed a few moments with all of them anytime she had the chance.

"John, those ladies are very special. Maybe we could invite them out for dinner some evening or something."

"Of course. We should do that . . . when?"

"I'll speak to Julia about it."

It was all settled without a problem, and in two weeks, as the daffodils were blooming, they smilingly came to dinner.

John stayed with them because he didn't feel like an outsider and was enjoying helping Janine with the meal and serving. The ladies seemed in high spirits to be there sharing time with one another.

When they left, the Stephenses were overflowing with joyful feelings and hopeful that they would have other opportunities to become better acquainted with these lovely ladies.

"How different they are from each other!" Janine said.

"Yes! I got a kick out of Beatrice. She's a real crackerjack!"

"She is! And so is Harriet, really. She surprised me a couple of times with her wit. We should have invited Ed Davidson and Owen Kendrick. I can't believe we didn't think to do that. I suppose the ladies had to fix dinner for their husbands before they even came here. What were we thinking?" Janine asked.

"It worked out all right. Iola is rather quiet, isn't she?"

"Yes, she thinks everything through obviously . . . And Anne is so capable with everything. They were talking about her sewing, her designing, and she is the treasurer of a couple of organizations."

"Well, I guess she taught mathematics. She *should* be the one to do the books," John said.

"I wish Rachael had been able to come—perhaps another time. Julia was so happy, John. I've never seen her smile so much! She was fascinated with our piano, but of course, she wouldn't go so far as to touch it . . . I told her to, but she just wouldn't."

"What was the name of the tall lady who sat opposite of you?"

"That's Adele Marsh—a beautiful person inside and out. Do you remember her at Bea's house at the October Fest?"

"I knew I had met her before! Yes, of course! What a group! Being with them reminds me of the scripture about many talents all working together. Everyone has something different to give to the whole. Don't you think?"

"Right! I noticed that too. It's very interesting, isn't it?"

"Yep. Well, it was a good idea, Janine. I think everyone left here feeling good about the evening. And it was very nice for us as well."

29

Philosophical

Janine could return to her early-morning time on the deck now that spring had arrived. The birds welcomed her back in full chorus, and the sun arrived on time every day. She felt that she was a real part of God's creation and not merely a spectator to the natural orchestration of the morning.

As she stood against the railing in meditation, she found herself lovingly considering Julia and the other "Ladies of Hope" as she often referred to them. She asked, "Lord, do they have hope? Are they looking forward and planning ahead, or have they adjusted to living each day as it comes and looking back upon the lives they have had?" Of course, she didn't expect an answer exactly.

"John, what would you say gives a person happiness?"

"Gee, hon, I suppose it would be defined differently for each person. Why do you ask? You're happy, aren't you?"

"Yes, I am. But happiness is not joy. Wouldn't you say that joy comes from God and happiness comes from something else?"

"Well, you're certainly being philosophical. What's on your mind?"

"Some people are happy because they have children or enjoy their work or because of where they live. Many people are simply void of unhappiness but are really not happy . . . I mean if you ask them if they are *un*happy they'll say no and be sure of it. But the truth is, they cannot search within themselves and say they are actually happy.

"They *would* be happy if they had someone to talk with each day or if they had something to look forward to or if their spouse were living or if their children actually lived nearby. There are many, many factors to this equation. Do you know what I'm saying?"

"Yes, I'm actually following you, believe it or not."

"Good." She felt encouraged to go on. "On the other hand, I think there are *very few* people who experience true joy except those who are in a full and direct relationship with the Lord.

"My question to you here is for the Ladies of Hope. I do believe that they have found peace and joy in Christ but that they are not experiencing a lot of happiness on a daily basis. Of course, having that relationship with Christ is far more important. As the Apostle Paul would say, 'It is everything.'"

"I agree."

"Yes, but as friends, supporters, and encouragers, we have opportunities to contribute happiness to the lives of others. I don't mean the 'joy' that is God-given, of course, but something that God's children can actually do for one another."

"Well, honey, I can't disagree with you on that, but where are you going with this?"

"I don't know."

"You don't know? Well, for goodness sakes. Why on earth are you going around about this with me?"

"I don't know. I really don't . . . I can't get this thought out of my mind."

"So . . . you're giving it to me?"

"No, not really . . . I just thought if I talked with you about it, I might get something from the conversation."

"But you didn't?"

"Nope . . . I guess I'll forget about it. At least I'll try. Thanks for listening."

She walked out of the room. He just stood there, wondering about her. One thing he knew for sure was that Janine was not going to forget about it. *When that girl gets something on her mind, she won't let it go until it's resolved. She'll find the answer she's looking for somehow.*

30

The Answer

Janine was reading Psalm 150 about praising God with instruments and reflected upon Julia's happiness playing the piano. Everybody enjoys music. *All of the Ladies of Hope would enjoy music, but not all of them will be playing the piano.* She had the answer! The answer was music.

She didn't say anything to John but went directly into the classroom on Sunday and said, "Ladies, how would you like to start a kitchen band?"

The immediate response was dead silence.

Finally, Beatrice asked, "What's that?"

"A kitchen band. You know!" Janine said.

"Why?" asked Iola.

Uh-oh! Janine had believed that the Lord wanted her to do this. But she hadn't done her part in researching. "Well, it will be fun. We'll get together once a week and . . . find some instruments from the kitchen . . . and have some time together, and then *go to lunch!* Maybe every Wednesday for a while."

Still silence; however, Janine did notice some little smiles when she said "Go to lunch." She should have done more preparation. Although she was a musician, she had never participated in a kitchen band—or any other band really. Now here she stood with egg on her face, wanting to do something for and with this remarkable group of ladies that would bring zest and fun into their lives, and she wasn't prepared to say the right things.

Anne was pondering what would be an easy way out of this. She was busy enough after all. She didn't want to hurt Janine's feelings, but she was one of the fortunate ones who still had her husband. She enjoyed her sewing, cooking, and had other interests and would not be participating. Pounding on pots and pans didn't sound like fun to her.

"I don't think I'll be able to do that, Janine. I have plenty to do to keep me busy," Anne said.

Iola nodded. *This is not the way I wish to spend my later years . . . What is she thinking? I'm the only one here who can even play a piano, except for Julia just learning. Surely she doesn't expect us to get together and, all of a sudden by some magic, make music.*

"I'm going to have to consider this for a while," Iola said. "I'm thinking that since we are 'church ladies,' if we are going to get together, we should probably study about what we can do for the church, for missions, or for our own understanding of the Bible in a new Bible study. How would that be?" Iola was glad she'd said it. After all, how frivolous to think of spending time being a kitchen band!

"Yes, Iola, that all sounds well and good. It really does, and I can't disagree with your thinking. But I believe that God is calling me to talk with you about having a good time. There is really nothing wrong with a little enjoyment."

Janine was struggling. Here were women who had decided they'd had enough fun in their lives, settling down into lives of acceptance. She remembered the special little book she had been given about joy. Actually when she'd read it, she had thought of her new friends here. There was a page in there . . . *Where did I put that book? Didn't I bring it to church last week? Wait! Wasn't it on the organ?* She wasn't ready to give up yet.

"I'll tell you what. Give it a little more thought. I have a few things to do, and if you don't mind, I'll come back and we can talk about this a little more." They nodded, and she was on her search for just the right things to say. Now this was risky and she knew it. They would all be discussing the absurdity of all this and reinforcing their earlier stance. She had to hurry. She found the book under a copy of the Doxology.

Okay now . . . where was that? I just read it the other day . . . Index. Let me see . . . No, no. That's not it. That's not it! Look some more. "The Joy of Enjoying Life." Yes, that's it here on page 19.

This was the final approach. It had better be good. *Lord, I believe you want me to do this. Help me, please.*

"Well, hello again. Before we discuss my proposition, please let me tell you about a writing in this little book. In part, it says we shouldn't miss life . . . It's a gift . . . We need to forget the practical sometimes—be zany and giddy."

She tried not to look up, but over the top of her glasses, she could see that "zany and giddy" did not go over very well. "Surprise yourself and enjoy the little things."

Janine continued, "This is really what I want you to do too. Give yourself permission to have fun. God wants us to enjoy our lives. We cannot always be studying, working, thinking. Sometimes we need a little recreation. I hope you will give this a try."

Julia knew Janine meant well, at least, and said, "I'm willing." It was quite a lot for Julia to say, never being one of the outspoken members of that class.

Beatrice always liked having fun. Actually, this sounded really good to her, and she was happy that Julia broke in and said she'd do it. "Hey! It's fine with me. I'm up for it . . . Let's do it. Will we meet this Wednesday?"

"Sure. We'll share our ideas. I think we can come up with some unique ideas from this group," Janine said. "Now, will the rest of you come Wednesday? Don't shut the door on it just yet."

Adele decided to go along with her good friend, Bea, even though she had no idea what she would be getting into. *It'll be something new and different. I could use a little diversion from the usual.*

"I guess I can make it," Adele said.

"Hey! I'll pick you up," Bea said, all smiles.

Harriet Burnett, the class teacher, said she would be traveling all summer, so it wouldn't make any sense to get started on something new.

Anne Kendrick, who had already said no, actually said she'd be there!

Everyone knew that Laura's husband was very ill. She would want to be with him, and she said so. Janine sensed that Laura needed a leisure activity, but all in God's time, she supposed.

The bell was ringing for Sunday school to end, and Janine was going to have to hurry to get things ready with her choir. "Well, I'd better get moving here."

Janine was very happy, but next time, she'd be prepared. In the meantime, she'd gather up some music and see if they had any good thoughts about what they might do. It was settled: Wednesday at 10:30 a.m., the pastor's day for visitations. Lunch would follow at the Orchard.

Thank You, Lord for helping me. This is certainly out of my line of work.

They met on Wednesday. Iola had not responded on Sunday, but she was there. Janine was thrilled at the turnout.

They had recruited Rachael, who was not presently attending the Sunday school class, but one whom they knew might enjoy a crafty meeting. Janine had recorded some old-fashioned tunes that each of the ladies knew from years past. They enjoyed the music and discussed what things from the kitchen might be used. The answer was "anything." They seemed happy at the end of the gathering and ready for lunch.

31

The Orchard Restaurant

It's too far to walk to the restaurant from the town, and no one would really want to walk along the two-lane road with today's traffic, so everyone piled into cars to go to lunch. Anne had announced that she would not be staying for lunch. Owen was getting along very well, but Anne always made it her priority not to stay away from home very long.

The restaurant, a part of Severight's Apple Orchard, had been in business for many years. Breakfast was ready at 5:00 a.m. for farmers who might be in, and there were always some who wouldn't miss the opportunity to discuss the business of farming or even the affairs of the government. They were strong in opinions and eager to talk.

This day, the lunch crowd was a few transients and not many locals. The farmers had much to do.

"Well, look who's here," Jackie said. "It's the ladies from Hope Church. What brings you out on a Wednesday? Are you having a Bible study?"

"Just a meeting," Iola spoke up quickly. She was not going to say *anything to anybody* about what they were doing. She thought it best to keep it all quiet. This band thing probably wouldn't last more than a week or two anyway.

No one else volunteered another word.

They went to a table in the back of the room. The ladies were apparently well acquainted with sitting there, and each gravitated to what seemed to be customary places around a table for eight. Rachael was given a seat at the end. Janine stood back a little and took an empty chair. Jackie was right behind them with her order pad.

"Have you met Janine, our organist?" asked Iola.

"I don't know if I have, actually. My name's Jackie. Nice to meet 'cha. Soup for today is stuffed pepper, chicken noodle, or vegetable beef."

"Is the chicken noodle fresh?" asked Rachael.

"Indeed it is. Virginia made it just this morning."

"Okay. I'll have a cup of that, a biscuit, and iced tea."

"I'll have a cup of vegetable soup. That will satisfy my vegetable requirement for the day," Iola said.

"You can't satisfy your vegetable requirement with a cup of soup," said Beatrice.

"Well, I think it's enough! I won't need any bread, and I'll have decaf coffee please."

"What kind of pie do you have?" asked Bea who always wants to be sure to leave room for her favorite if they have it.

"Peach, Dutch apple, caramel apple, lemon meringue, raisin, and chocolate," said Jackie.

"Well, in that case, I'll skip the soup and have a piece of that caramel apple with vanilla ice cream. Coffee too, please . . . regular."

"I really like the stuffed pepper soup. I'll have the white bowl of soup," Adele Marsh said. "And just iced water, please."

"What's the white bowl?" asked Janine.

"It's the medium-sized bowl," responded Jackie.

"I'm pretty hungry. I'll take the regular-sized bowl of vegetable beef soup, please, and a cup of regular coffee . . . black."

Everyone else ordered, and in no time, the food arrived. The soups must have been hot in the pots.

"A cup of soup for Iola, one for Rachael, the white bowl for Adele, Bea gets the pie, Miss Julia a bacon sandwich on toast, and a bowl of soup for Janine. Right?"

Everyone looked at Janine and her bowl of soup. My goodness, it was enough to serve a family! This must be a farmer's bowl. She was embarrassed to have so much set before her and told the ladies she had no idea it would be so large. Jackie asked if she would like to have her take it back, and she said, "Oh no. That's fine. I'll know better next time. It's certainly not your fault." She'd eat what she could.

Well, it was so good she could have eaten it all, but now she wouldn't because she had made such a fuss about the portion in the beginning.

They talked very little about what had transpired that morning, concerned that someone might hear them discussing such things; however, Pauline Johnston's name was mentioned to one who should have been contacted to be a part of this group. Of course! She was attending our church now and was a distant cousin of Bea's by marriage. This was a great suggestion as it turned out. Pauline loved theater and loves being on stage, and since she was now alone, she might want to try meeting with the others.

"I don't know her very well. How old is she?" Julia asked.

"Oh, she's at least eighty," Beatrice said, "which puts her right in the same age bracket as the rest of us. I'll call her today when I get home."

"Good idea," Julia said.

"Thanks, everyone, for coming out today. We'll get it all figured out, and when we do, it's going to be such fun," Janine said outside of the restaurant. There were a few people over at one of the tables in the back who knew these were women from Hope Church and were very curious as to what they were up to.

Everyone got into a car and drove off, vowing to be back together next Wednesday. No one was happier than Janine. *What a fantastic group of women. They have years of wisdom and deserve special playful moments in their lives. It's a blessing for me to have this opportunity to get to know them better.*

Thank You, Lord, for bringing me to Julia who has helped to open doors for me here in West Hope. As time moved forward, she would know full well that it was all part of the Plan.

32

The Band

A few weeks later, they entered the church and took out the supplies they would be using. Janine had some music books, kazoos, and a large red plastic spoon that she would use as the director's baton. She gave each lady a kazoo.

What in the world?

Finally, Julia spoke up. "What is this anyway?"

"Oh. It's a kazoo. We'll be attaching one to each of our instruments and play along," said Janine.

She had no idea that they were totally perplexed as to which end was which and how to use it at all. She'd soon find out.

In the meantime, Julia had those very pretty aprons to share. They each chose one, put it on, and thought they were very nice, which pleased Julia. In earlier days, Julia had sewn many things. These were part of her collection of hostess aprons. Some had flowered embroidery, a few had rickrack covering from the waist down. They had certainly never been used for cooking. That would not have been practical of course. A cooking-style apron covers from neck to knee and is always removed when greeting guests or serving the meal.

Adele had a great-looking "violin" made from a polished wood spoon that she said hung on her kitchen wall. She had made a bridge for it, attached four strings, and brought a small round curtain rod for the bow.

"Do you think this would work?" she asked. Adele was tall, stately, and everyone agreed that she was the perfect person to play a violin. She placed the violin under her chin and drew the bow across. The gals were extremely impressed.

Iola had a bottle brush with colorful, curly ribbons attached and said that she would put her kazoo on it. Janine was pleased. She knew Iola better today. And she actually found her to be quite reserved, which limited her ability to relax and be comfortable participating in anything the least bit silly. She was a good woman, always fulfilling her responsibilities properly and without flair—not a person who needed entertainment or frivolous moments. It was truly an effort for her to be meeting like this as she wasn't sure that it was the proper thing to do. But she was trying.

She and Janine attached the kazoo to the handle of the brush with masking tape. Iola had perfect pitch and, in no time, was humming through the kazoo . . . ever so softly.

Rachael reached down into one of her bags and pulled out a "trumpet" that she had made for Anne. Apparently, she had discussed this with Anne over the telephone, and Anne seemed eager to receive it. What a trumpet! It was a small plunger sprayed with shiny brass paint. Rachael had glued three thimbles for the keys that were perfect for Anne because of her sewing abilities. Everyone was amazed at such an idea.

Janine had never dreamed that a plunger could be used as an instrument, but leave it to Rachael! She had surprised them again with her creativity.

Anne, who was generally very quiet about everything, expressed her delight and appreciation to Rachael. *Once I have it mastered, I will stand tall and be a trumpeter!* She had mastered many things in the past with her sewing, public speaking, and other skills. This band thing was all new to her, but she was ready for the challenge. She would give it her best.

The ladies were beginning to look at everything in the kitchen, the stores, yard sales, etc., as a potential musical instrument. Their creativity was profuse, and their ideas amazed Janine.

Beatrice had a whisk, Julia a slotted spoon, Rachael had an eggbeater, and they each applied the kazoos. It was not so easy for those three. They tried blowing through the kazoos and were totally unsuccessful in producing anything other than wind. Iola confidently took on the responsibility of teaching Bea, Julia, Rachael, and Anne the proper way of voicing the instruments. After several failed attempts and much laughter from the students, they soon were humming along with Iola.

Beatrice enjoyed laughter. She was older than everyone except Julia and yet was clearly younger in spirit than any in the group. She was always looking for ways to bring delight and laughter into the group. She danced around the room with her kazoo, thoroughly enjoying the fact that she was making music. Nothing held her back, and she was the free spirit that everyone deep inside truly longed to be.

They were practicing to be a kitchen band. Janine looked at them having such a good time of it. She could not have envisioned this.

ᘐᘐᘐ

On Wednesday, Anne suggested that they put chairs in a row and stand or sit and play the songs. They played "Bicycle Built for Two" standing and looking pretty fine, and when some of them put on the aprons, a "band" began to emerge.

Janine recalled a line in Psalm 126 that she had read for the morning devotions:

> The Lord hath done great things for us;
> whereof we are glad.

She had repeated that small verse to herself all morning and recited it to them. They nodded their heads in apparent understanding.

Janine noticed when they were at the Orchard Restaurant that day, they couldn't stop talking about the band, and they didn't seem to care if anyone heard them. Some of the usual customers and waitresses were wondering what the chatter was all about and what was causing them to be so full of laughter and giggles.

The ladies of the band were still the lovely, amazing ladies they had always been, but now, there was cheerfulness that was noticeable by everyone. The ladies were coming to Sunday school, talking with excitement about a new idea, a new instrument, or a new song.

Pauline Johnston would be joining them when she returned from her visit with her family in Michigan, so they were growing in many ways.

Janine asked Harriet Burnett, the Sunday school teacher, if she was able to get the lesson across with so much discussion about the band. She responded, as any good librarian would, "Absolutely."

It was not unusual for Beatrice or Rachael or any of the others to tell Janine that they had something new to bring to practice the following Wednesday. Their minds were buzzing with creativity, and they discovered that they were energized and walking with a rhythm.

33

Silas

Janine and Julia pulled up to the curb in front of Julia's house.

"Julia, who cuts your grass? It looks very nice today."

"Oh, the local 'handyman' comes every so often and takes care of whatever. Most of us widows need some help now and then, and he's good at most things around. His name is Silas. He lives out Ridge Road and into the countryside somewhere. He comes around every so often, and most of us just wait until someone sees him working at a place and then we let him know we need some work done, and so forth. It all works out."

"I don't think I've ever seen him."

"Maybe not. Iola thinks he comes by when he runs out of money because he's on no kind of schedule at all."

"How long have you known him? Is he trustworthy?" Janine asked.

"I guess he is. I never heard anyone complain about him. The truth is, I don't know much about Silas. He doesn't talk much, won't eat anything offered, drinks a little glass of water now and then, and that's about all of the real face-to-face contact I ever have with him."

"How old is he?"

"Hmm . . . maybe sixty. I don't know really. He's tall and thin. He seems to have trouble with a hip or something. He could be younger with a bad hip or older with arthritis. It's hard to say."

"Well, I must say, I wish you knew more about him. You can't be too careful, you know."

"Oh, around here, people are pretty nice. Don't worry about Silas. He's been a part of the community for a long time. He goes to help Iola and a couple of others in the borough. He used to help out Jenny before she moved to the suburbs. He's fine. Pastor Daniel likes him. He goes out to visit with him but keeps it all confidential. Apparently, Silas wants to keep to himself, so we don't question that. Can't help but wonder about him though. If we knew he needed anything, we'd all want to help, but he is so quiet about himself, and no one knows for sure."

"Does he have a lawn mower?"

"I guess not. He always used mine and anybody else's. When he finishes up, he comes to the back door and says, 'Will you need anything else done today, Mrs. Gillanders?' And I'll usually say, 'Well, I think not today, Silas.' Or I might say, 'I was wondering if you'd like to take a look at this leaky sink (or whatever).' And he'd say, 'Yes, ma'am.'

"If he has an old cap on, he'll take it off, wipe his shoes on the rug, and take a look at the problem. One day, he did look at the drip in the kitchen, tried to turn the water off, and said, 'Well, that frazzlin' thing won't budge.' He went to his old truck and came back with a great big tool of some kind, clamped it on someway, gave it a twist and a grunt, and that was that! It was fixed.

"Then he said, 'Anything else, ma'am?' I said, 'I guess that's it for today.' I paid him for the grass cutting and asked him about his charge for fixing the sink. He said, 'Oh, anything or nothing at all would be fine. T'weren't much to it.'

"I gave him a few extra dollars, and he put the money in his pocket without looking at it and said, 'Thanks, Mrs. Gillanders. I'll see you next time.'

"And that was that. Usually when he is here, if anyone else needs him, they'll call me up and tell me to tell Silas to stop by when he finishes here. That's how he works."

Janine was thinking lots of things she would not say at this time. Apparently, he had built up a reputation that was satisfactory with the neighborhood. As for herself, she'd like to know more about him. But if that's the "way he works," she'd have to let it rest there for now.

She saw Julia to the door and left for home.

34

Treasures

One Tuesday morning, Julia announced that right after lessons she wanted to take Janine to meet someone. What a thrill it was when that someone turned out to be Emery Oller, a well-known and exceptional artist. Janine was flabbergasted. She didn't know that Mr. Oller was living in that tiny town. Actually, his home was not on the main street but out of town, over Ridge Road and on the other side of the hill, tucked in where he could afford complete privacy. He was quite the gentleman. He showed Janine his studio and his works in progress.

He had moved to the community from life in a big city to be away from the hustle-bustle. He said he had painted landscapes for years and was always drawn to West Hope and the outlying area. Many years ago, he had decided that this would be the home of his later years. He and his wife found this little house tucked away and knew immediately that they were exactly where they belonged. His wife, Susan, a lovely and quiet lady, had developed beautiful perennial gardens and enjoyed showing them to Janine.

Her lilies were impressive. She had several varieties in many beautiful colors. Janine said, "Last summer, we gathered up some orange ones from along a creek near our home and planted. Actually, I had no idea there were all of these different types. Amazing and beautiful! Thank you for sharing with me. I seem to be learning new things each and every day. It's absolutely wonderful!"

Janine couldn't believe her good fortune to have been introduced to these two very talented and inspiring people.

His studio was a very large room, perhaps thirty feet by twenty, with a skylight overhead and many windows. As they entered the room, Janine immediately smelled the oils and paints, and was swept away with a sense of being in a very special place.

Emery had been painting for decades, and his works were magnificent. He took the time to discuss his techniques (not entirely understood by Janine) and showed her some sketches and paintings. She couldn't stop asking him questions, and he was very gracious to answer them all. Julia and Susan stayed in the house while Janine visited the studio with Emery. It was a day to remember for the rest of her life.

"Julia, how can I ever thank you? This was a thrill for me."

"He is a friend. I wanted both of you to meet each other."

Janine was quite stirred by the experience. She could hardly wait to tell her husband about the unexpected event. John was cutting grass in the lower yard when she arrived at the house. She made some cold tea, and when he came in and cooled off a bit, she told him of her day. He was always happy to have Janine share the experiences she had with the ladies of the band and of special moments with Julia. "Janine, you have stumbled upon a treasure in Julia."

"I have, John, but it was not a stumble. It was part of the Plan."

John smiled knowingly as he understood exactly what she meant. The Plan—God's Plan has been much better than any plan either of them ever had, and they are seeing it more clearly every day.

35

Rachael's Hospitality

On Sunday after church, Rachael invited the ladies to come to her house for lunch after band practice. Janine thought that was so nice, and she offered to take something to eat.

"No, no. That won't be necessary. I'm really looking forward to entertaining once again. I used to have people in quite often, but during these past years, I haven't felt well enough to do it. I'm so happy to be feeling up to it again. I'm planning on two soups, some salad foods, breads, and pie. Will that be enough?"

"Goodness, yes! You are unbelievable, Rachael. When we first met, you had just gotten onto your feet from your terrible accident. Are you sure about this?"

"Janine, you don't know what I've been through. Twice the church prayed me back from near death. I wouldn't even be here today without their prayers. And this time was the same thing. I don't know why anyone wants me to go on living, but they won't let me go yet. God must want me here for some reason that is completely unknown to me."

She continued, "I've had a good life. I had the best husband in the world. We enjoyed learning about farming together when we bought the farm early in our marriage. We loved it here so much that we've always wanted to share it with everyone. We often had children come for school field trips. I'd bake cookies and make lemonade, and they would learn a little about farm life.

"My own children have stayed around here, thankfully. Their friends always came home with them after school, and I would fix them special treats or even have them stay for dinner. I'm quite used to having folks in. Of course, it's just a tiny house, but it's fun to fill it up."

There was that beautiful, broad smile lighting up Rachael's face that Janine had become accustomed to, and she knew there would be no possibility of changing her mind. Rachael would do it all.

ϓ ϓ ϓ

The ladies all seemed excited to be going to Rachael's house, and Janine drove Julia, Bea, and Adele. They drove out a small country road and turned to drive to the top of one of the many hills of the community. The drive was steep and unpaved, and although Julia still drove, she would not want to go it alone to Rachael's, especially after the morning rain. They were having no problems negotiating today. Actually, the road had completely dried. Fields of ripening hay were waving in the breeze, bending gently to and fro on each side of the narrow drive. The car engine stirred up a rabbit, and they noticed a red-winged blackbird sitting on a fence post, obviously keeping watch over its nest of young.

Janine had picked up Rachael for practices but had not been inside the house, which looked barely larger than perhaps four rooms. She was right. There was an entrance with two rooms to the left and two to the right. The entrance had a stairway to the upper floor, but she imagined that there would not be more than an attic-type room there. How quaint! It was like a little cottage in the woods from the childhood stories her mother had read to her, but this little house sat atop of the hill overlooking great pastures and hills in the distance.

She was led into the sitting room on the right. There were the others of the band except for two who had gone off into the kitchen with Rachael. Janine and her companions sat down with the others and looked around and talked about one thing or another.

There were figurines, vases, lamps, doilies, and pictures. It was a beautiful room full of a lifetime of interesting collectables. Within a few minutes, everyone was invited to go to the dining room. What a beautiful surprise! The table was set with fine china, silverware, linen tablecloth and napkins, and a beautiful centerpiece. There were condiments on the table in lovely crystal dishes. The water glasses were full of ice and water, and the corners of the tablecloth were gathered up and tied with ribbons and flowers that matched the centerpiece.

Perfect!

The breads were brought out from the kitchen along with salads. Adele was helping, and she looked beautiful as she always did, serving each person from the right as she no doubt had learned well.

Rachael asked if anyone would like to ask the blessing, and again, Adele stepped forward to her request.

"Father in heaven, we bow before You on this wonderful occasion to give You thanks for Your many blessings. We thank You for bringing us together in love and fellowship and enjoyments. Bless each and every one of those gathered here. Lord, we pray Your blessings upon this home and the one who has so graciously invited us to it. Bless the food we are about to eat. May we be strengthened, Lord, to do Your will today and always. We ask in Jesus's name. Amen."

Everyone said "Amen."

Janine was thinking, *Did she actually say "for bringing us together in love, fellowship, and enjoyments?" Are we getting there? Oh Lord, thank You.*

Rachael was speaking. "Janine . . . Janine."

"Oh, sorry. I was thinking of something, I guess."

"Would you like chicken noodle soup or navy bean?"

"I'll have the regular-sized bowl of navy bean." Everyone caught the joke and had a good laugh over it. It felt so good to be relaxed enough to laugh at herself with them.

They talked about the morning's practice. Beatrice had brought in Mexican hats for everyone. What a hoot! They had put them on, modeled them around, and ended up in a row, emulating a hat dance. They had such a good time. Each forgot that she was not supposed to be "giddy and zany." Janine would never tell them that they were in fact being just that! Cha-cha-cha!

But now, what were they going to do with the hats? Janine suggested they might make maracas for the next meeting. She knew they would be creative. She would never attempt to outguess them.

The day ended on a very high note. Rachael was the perfect host, the food was delicious, the friendships were deepening, and joy abounded. They were developing into a sisterhood, sharing one another's joys and burdens, and feeling the bonds of love tighten.

36

Cha-Cha-Cha

Janine recorded "La Cucaracha." She figured out a dance routine that the band members could do in a line, laughing and enjoying all that involved. She moved around the house as she listened to the music.

John came in and caught her being lighthearted and silly. He was so pleased to see her happy and so relaxed.

"Well, well. What have we here?" he asked, grabbing her and whirling her around the kitchen. They almost fell over together, laughing like two children, and when the music stopped, she shouted, "*Olé!*"

When had the mood in their home shifted from the days of minute-by-minute scheduling and tension to fun and games again? *This is so much better,* she thought and gave John a big hug, which he generously returned.

ϒϒϒ

Pauline came to her first practice without an instrument. She wasn't sure what to expect. She enjoyed every minute of being together with the group. She needed the fellowship of the sisterhood and was ready to begin.

Pauline was living alone in a nearby community in the neighborhood of her childhood. Unfortunately, everyone she had known was gone. Pauline, now a widow, refused to become depressed. She knew she needed to keep busy and set up an art studio in her apartment. She jumped right in, gathered some of her previous supplies, added new ones, and began painting again for the first time in many years.

She loved the process but would not attempt to sell any of her works. If someone liked a painting she had completed, she would give it to that person. Many very fortunate friends and relatives now had paintings on their walls that have been admired over the years.

She went home, turned up her creativity full force, and designed a trombone and set out to figure a way to put it together. She determined she could use brass curtain rods and acquired those from a neighbor. With her husband's old soldering iron, she joined the pieces together and attached the curtain rods together in a sliding position. She added a large funnel for the mouth and a potato-chip clip for aid in sliding, and yes, it actually slid! She spray-painted the entire instrument in a brass finish, and by the next week, she had it ready for practice. She made it all sound so easy! Well, maybe to her, but not so easy for the others. When she walked into the practice with the trombone, everyone thought it was real.

Wednesday, the week after Rachael's lunch, the band members came in full of life and excitement. Everyone had maracas. They might have talked about it between themselves, but Janine was totally surprised. Pauline had two tin Slim-Fast cans with beans inside and the top was still on them. *How on earth?* She probably had soldered them as she had her trombone instrument. They were great!

Adele had soup cans with various beans inside. She had applied some kind of top to each can. They made a super sound.

Julia had soup cans also and had taped the tops closed.

Rachael had Coca-Cola cans with little stones rattling inside. Bea and Iola each had Ensure cans. Anne had some kind of nutritional supplement cans. What a hoot! All these had the pop-top tabs, so they had inserted the noisemakers inside and closed the tabs. Neat idea. Actually, Janine thought the nutritional cans were zany and pointing fun at themselves, but she sure wasn't going to say anything like that to them!

They put on the hats, held the maracas up in front, one in each hand, and Janine taught them the routine. They loved it. They went over it several times, and they were willing to do so. At the end, Janine yelled, "*Olé!*" Everyone in the band responded "*Olé!*" and lifted up their arms.

Perfect!

37

Carry Your Light into the World

"Saints alive!" The band has been invited to perform in public! One of the larger churches in the denomination would be installing a new pastor, and they invited the band to be the after-dinner entertainment. This certainly changed everything. No one expected to go out and entertain. All they wanted was to have fun together. Of course, they had gotten very polished with their songs, and someone has let the cat out of the bag.

On the second Wednesday in August, the band got together for another reason: to decide if this is the direction it should go. As shocking as it was, it should be considered.

Janine stopped for Julia and Rachael and met the others at the church. One would hardly recognize the band anymore. They had all kinds of hats and matching aprons! They had a trombone, a trumpet, and several other instruments that they cannot name that came from the kitchen. They even had a routine. Were they prepared to go into the world?

Janine took the members of the band to the church fellowship hall, sat them down, and said, "Ladies, you have an invitation to perform at the Second Church in Harperton for the installation of their minister. Let's talk about it."

"Oh my goodness, we can't do that," said Adele. "We just aren't good enough to do such a thing."

"And we are far, far too silly to be out in public," voiced Anne.

"What are they thinking to even consider us for such a serious situation as the installation of a pastor?" asked Iola.

"I don't know how they found out about us," said Janine. "Does anyone know?"

"Well, everyone at our church knows what we are doing. Even though they haven't seen us, I'm sure the word is out by now," Bea said. "Exactly who invited us?"

"I have the invitation here . . . It was Sarah Brooks."

"Well . . . I did tell her about the band. We talk almost every day," Bea admitted.

"I guess I told her also," Rachael said. "I said to her that she should be in our band. We have so much fun. She and I have been friends for a long time."

Janine said, "Ladies, I realize that this is a very scary thought, but whether you know it or not, you are truly a unique and wonderful band, and I don't think you can hide your light under a bushel for much longer. Don't you think that people might actually enjoy your talents and creativity?"

"Our silliness, you mean."

"My goodness! We have reputations to uphold."

"We are properly reared people. Others respect us for that. We can't just go out there acting like clowns!"

"I have to tell you, this might just be part of the Plan. Think about that. Can God call us together in His name—and He has—and not expect more of us than just meeting to have fun among ourselves forever? I think we all believed that was why we came together here. I sure did! It was what I wanted for you. But I now can see that I wanted that because God put it in my heart, and He has a larger role for you. You can witness His love through your talents. Yes, your *talents!* I don't know if you realize just how special you are."

Janine was stunned at what she was saying. What was God asking her to do? These words were not even hers. She didn't rehearse these words to say today.

The ladies were so disturbed at the thought that they couldn't say anything for a good while. Finally, Rachael spoke up, "You know what? She's right. We are good, and we should share what we have found with other people."

Everyone wanted to agree . . . Everyone was afraid to do so.

"I'll tell you what. Let's set up a routine, go through it, changing our hats, instruments, working it all out, and then see if we can come to some conclusion here," Janine suggested.

Well, they could go that far, at least.

"How about if we march in? We could have chairs lined up with our bags of changes alongside of each chair. You could go out of sight with a marching instrument, the laughable hats that you made for yourselves, and your apron. When you march in, you will not be Rachael, Bea, Anne, etc., you will be *The Kitchen Band.* What do you say to that?"

"Well, we can do that today, but can't we be called something else beside *The Kitchen Band?*" Pauline asked.

"Like what?"

"I don't know. But we should think about it."

Janine suggested that would be a good question to ponder over the week and discuss it the next time. They all agreed.

"Can we go ahead and set up the chairs and bags? Once you are comfortable with having everything at your fingertips, take your supplies to the door and be prepared to march in according to the lineup of the chairs. Pauline, will you lead us in with your trombone?" Pauline had no inhibitions and agreed readily.

"All right, now let's see what we can do. Just follow my lead as to which song will be next."

After everyone was ready, Janine picked up the tambourine made from a round cake pan, turned on the music to a zippy marching tune, and beckoned the band to enter. They were making music through their kazoos and looking great too. They followed Janine's direction as to the next selections and discovered that they had an actual routine.

They were relaxing and enjoying themselves after awhile. They even danced to "La Cucaracha" with their maracas. They were surprised when they realized that they were doing a sufficiently decent job of performing.

"Well?" Janine looked at them for answers.

"We can do it," said Anne. *Anne?* Astonishingly, they all agreed.

Now they were a band with a mission and a purpose—one that was called by God to witness His love to others. What can make a believer happier? What can give life more meaning?

Naturally, Janine was not sure what they were thinking. Private expressions could not be exposed and shared among the group just yet—those thoughts that were hidden in their hearts that day and the questions that had arisen would one day be fully answered.

Can we actually be productive and helpful? Can this be real?

Does God still have something for us to do?

I can't believe it! Look at us! We are old and yet God has not closed the door.

Sarah was old . . . Noah was old . . . They served God's purpose, and so can I!

Everything changed from that moment.

ᴕᴕᴕ

Driving home, Janine decided to go on down the lane to Kathy's and visit for a while.

Kathy heard her drive up and so did Prince. Kathy came out of the front door, smiling.

"Well, hi there," she said. "I'm glad to see you. What's up?"

"Oh, I'm just on my way home from a kitchen band rehearsal and thought I'd stop over for a few minutes."

"Great. Come on in. The girls are visiting friends today, and I'm home alone right now. Let's sit down with a glass of lemonade."

"Mmm . . . That sounds perfect. It's a very warm day."

They went inside, and it was nice and cool. A home built of logs provided great natural insulation against the heat, and the ceiling fans were all that was needed. They walked back through the great room to the expansive kitchen. Kathy had freshly squeezed lemonade in the refrigerator, and they sat down at the breakfast table to chat.

"Something's on your mind, Mother. What is it?"

"Well, you're right, of course. You always know, don't you?"

"I guess so." She was blessed that she and her daughter lived near enough to each other to be able to meet and talk. They were so close. Janine was very close in spirit with Deborah also, thus she felt doubly blessed. Prince curled up at her feet as though to say "We're listening."

"The band practice went very well. Kathy, things have turned out beyond my expectations. Well, in truth, I didn't really *have* any expectations. So no matter what they would have done in the way of creativity would have been more than I expected . . . But here's the thing. We've been invited to entertain somewhere. We have talked about it, and after lots of thinking it through, we decided we would do it."

"Oh, my heavens, Mother . . . . What on earth are you thinking? The ladies are not musicians. They are not actresses or performers or anything of the sort. They are just having fun. You can't do this. You will ruin their reputations. You will upset the applecart. They will never be able to face anyone again."

"Kathy, settle down now. I wouldn't suggest that they do anything that would embarrass them. You just don't understand. They really are good at what they are doing."

"And what's that? Making fools of themselves? Mother, please! I know you love the ladies. Think of them. Are you thinking of *them?* They will be embarrassed. They will!" She stood up and walked back and forth.

"Oh my goodness, Mother! I absolutely can't believe that you are considering such a thing."

"Kathy, if you could see how happy they are and what joy they could bring to others, you'd understand. I believe that God has called them to go into the world and share the joy they have found. They will be an inspiration to others and an encouragement to the older generation to participate in life."

"I know that's what you think, but what if it doesn't go that way? Who invited you to entertain anyway?"

"Second Church of Harperton. They want us to be the entertainment after dinner when the new pastor is being installed."

Kathy plopped down into the chair and grabbed her head in both hands. "Merciful heavens! This is worse than I thought! Mother, that's a very formal and meaningful event in the life of the church. Why on earth would they want The Kitchen Band? They should get a nice choral group or something like that."

"Kathy, please. You should just come and sit in on a rehearsal. I know it's hard to believe that those beautiful, respectable ladies who have always been exceedingly prim and proper could possibly be enjoying themselves by clowning around, but they do. And when they are working together, a spark ignites that communicates energy and vitality. I'm sure it will all come across. I'm putting it in God's hands."

"Well, I hope He sees it the way you think He does."

"I'm sure He will. Kathy, will you pray with me? Will you release those feelings of anxiety and pray with me that God will be with us and help us to do the work He wants us to do?"

"Mother, you know I want to." She stood and walked around the kitchen again, saying nothing. She walked around the island counter, at times shaking her head, with a troubled look on her face. Janine knew she was trying to release those feelings.

Finally, Kathy sat down with her mother, took her hands and said, "Mother, I love you so much. You have such a deep conviction and are so close to the Lord. I trust that you have made the right decision. Let's pray together."

They bowed in prayer and asked the Lord for guidance, courage, strength, and help for the band members. They asked the Lord for the audience to embrace the band with love and that the band would bring glory to the Father as they shared His love with others.

When they finished, Kathy stood up and embraced her mother. "Mother, I've never known you to do anything to hurt anybody, and I'm sorry that I jumped on you like that. Is there anything I can do to help the band get ready? Can I help you load up, set up, or something?"

Janine felt relief and release. Kathy was helpful, as she knew she would be, and it strengthened Janine to have her support too. "Well, you could come along with us and give us a hand if you really want to. That would be just great."

"Sure. I can do that. When is the installation?"

They talked about the logistics of it all, and Janine said she really should be getting on over to her own home. She hugged Kathy again, thanked her for her loyalty and support, patted Prince, and was on her way.

ᵧᵧᵧ

"What will we wear?" Iola was asking.

The rest of the band members were waiting for some kind of answer. Well, Janine had always pictured them in cotton housedresses with their aprons.

"I don't have a housedress," Bea said.

"Neither do I," said Adele.

"Could you wear cotton skirts with a blouse then?" asked Janine.

"I think we should wear slacks," said Iola.

"Well, you are a kitchen band. Seems to me a skirt with an apron would go together nicely," Janine replied.

"I'd rather wear slacks," said Iola.

"Me too." The others all agreed.

Janine was stunned. She never in her wildest dreams thought that these women from the older generation would prefer to go out in public wearing pants. She actually had a hard time even picturing it.

"Well, I suppose it's okay, if that's what you want to do," she said.

"What color?" asked Julia.

"How about black?" Adele responded.

"I don't have black." Julia's response surprised Janine. Everyone surely has black.

"Neither do I," said Anne. Does everybody have navy blue?"

This was getting to be a challenge. They finally all agreed on the navy blue with a white blouse. Janine didn't think they needed to match, but they certainly thought they should. So be it.

As director, she would not be obliged to dress the same, so she would figure it out later. She had planned to discuss a name for the band; however, after all the discussion concerning apparel, she decided not to bring it up. Perhaps they would forget about that.

They rehearsed for the last time, added a little more conversation, went over the time schedule and drivers, and they did forget about the name.

38

A Step of Faith

John positively had to go see this performance! Janine was happy that he felt that way, and she and John and Kathy stopped by for Julia and Rachael. Transportation had been arranged for the others . . . Harperton was not very far. They would all meet at the fellowship hall and set up everything on the stage (*good grief!*) before the installation ceremony. Julia and Rachael were chatting about the band in the backseat with Kathy enjoying the conversation.

They all arrived at nearly the same time and parked in specially marked spaces around the back. Janine knocked on the locked door, and someone was waiting for them, offering to lend a hand. John and Kathy also helped, and in no time, the chairs were set up on the stage, the instruments were in their chosen places, and their aprons and hats were within reach. Janine needed a table to put the sound equipment on, which was a bit of a problem. A worse problem arose when no one knew where to find extension cords. Janine had not considered that.

John went looking for a janitor or trustee while Janine sorted through her bag to be sure she had things in order. She had the CD and her list. *Good. Okay, now, what to do about electricity?* Eventually after what seemed like an eternity and the ceremony in the sanctuary was about to begin, a young man came running in with enough cords to light up a holiday room with several Christmas trees. Janine plugged her sound equipment in, tested it, and when all was well, they entered the sanctuary.

What a lovely service. All the top officials of the district were there to assist. *All the top officials!* Her heart stopped momentarily. She should have thought ahead. She knew that they would be there, of course, but hadn't thought about it. Now here she was with her band without a name, presenting themselves before the public for the first time, and the place was loaded up with top guns! She thought she would faint and suddenly realized that would be advantageous.

Okay. That would be fine. They'd carry me out on a stretcher, and everyone would understand that we would have to back out of doing the entertainment this evening. We would all be so sorry, and everyone could show their extreme disappointment at not being able to follow through, but what could we do after all?

She didn't faint. Instead, she was standing and singing with the congregation. The new pastor was so charming, and everyone seemed very pleased to have her. This would be a turning point for this congregation with a woman pastor. Times were changing for sure.

The service was over, and everyone was filing into the fellowship hall, pushing the members of the band along whether they wanted to go or not! A few people came up to them and said that they were looking forward to hearing them.

I wish they'd not say that, thought Janine. She looked for her support at Kathy, who grabbed her hand and said that the Lord was with her. "Do your best for Him," she said. She always seemed to say the right things. Janine felt better and tried to concentrate on the great meal that had been prepared. She even ate some of it, to her surprise, but she could not eat any dessert. It would surely stick in her throat.

Sarah Brooks came up to her, all smiles. She didn't know Sarah until she introduced herself. "We are so excited, Janine. Thank you so much for coming."

"Sarah, it's good to meet you. Thanks for inviting us. I suppose it was inevitable that we would begin our ministry soon. I'm happy that you gave us a little push."

"Do you need anything, Janine?" asked Sarah.

"I think if I had a microphone, it would help. I didn't realize how large this room would be, and we want those in the back to hear the conversations between the band members."

"No problem. I'll get someone on it right away. We have just a few things to do before the entertainment and then we'll be ready. Okay?"

"Absolutely," Janine said. *Absolutely. Absolutely. Maybe she'd faint after all!*

"Ladies, we will want to go ahead and get up to the stage." Showing confidence, she said, "Let's go do it."

They all moved in the right direction at least. Each would get her supplies and go out of the room. Janine would put on a smile and tell a little about the band and turn on the music. She could do that; she had it rehearsed well.

Janine had spoken before people many times as the announcer for concerts, dinners, and even as president of local community affairs, but this was different! *Why?* She just couldn't figure out why at the moment. She didn't have time to figure out why. Sarah was introducing her! Everybody was clapping. *Will they be clapping later?*

She said a short prayer for help, turned to face the audience, and saw Kathy and John beaming with encouragement. She smiled and said, "Hello, everyone. I greet you in the name of Jesus Christ Who has called our band together to go into the world in His name to show His love and spread His joy. As Sarah has told you, we come from West Hope. Every member of the band has been at that church for many years. And I do mean, 'many.'

"I am eager for you to meet one of the most unique bands ever assembled. There is no other band like this one. First of all, please know that the members designed every instrument that they are playing tonight, and every instrument came from the kitchen. That was our only criteria. The key has been creativity, and they have an overabundance of that.

"Will you help me bring out the band?" She began to clap and so did the audience. The music started, and there they were. They came out of the kitchen, of course, marching to the music. The audience continued to clap to the music and never faltered in its enthusiasm for the band. That enthusiasm covered the band with love. It was the answer to a prayer.

The band held up and did a decent job. The audience thought they were better than that. As they continued with the program, the folks laughed, even the big guns, and the new pastor was having a wonderful time.

The band finished with "La Cucaracha," dancing right through it while shaking the maracas. Bea especially liked the song, and put in some extra shaking with her body movements. Everyone loved it. "*Olé!*"

The audience was on its feet! They had made their début without falling on their faces. Hallelujah!

Janine looked out at the audience of smiles and then to John and Kathy who were smiling through tears and clapping harder than anyone else.

Kathy came up to her mother, embraced her, and said, "Now I understand."

Janine turned to the ladies, saw their smiles, and said to Kathy, "And now—so do I."

The End

Addendum

The story will continue in the third book of the West Hope trilogy with Janine and her family, sharing laughter and tears as relationships intensify in their newfound community and "the band plays on." Janine and the ladies recognize with certainty that God's Plan is not only for their happiness but that the band is to be used for a higher purpose. They are challenged to venture forth to entertain and raise the spirits and hopes of others.

As the word spreads about the entertainment quality of The Kitchen Band, they receive invitations to interesting and sometimes unusual places, including a nationally broadcast television show in a large city . . . but how far should they go?

Read more about the faithfulness and extended hope of the residents of West Hope and surrounding communities in Mary Jean's final book of the trilogy and of the love and joy in the sisterhood of the band as "the band plays on."